"Would you like me to walk you over to Penny's?"

Tara shook her head. "I'
watch me walk across the
feel better."

Glen ran his fingers through his hair. He thought the offer to walk with her might ease some of the tension between them. Ever since he'd told Tara about his date with Sinda, she'd been irritable. He straightened his tie and smoothed the lapel on his gray sport coat. "Do I look okay? I'm not overdressed, am I?"

"I guess it all depends on where you're goin'," Tara answered curtly. She sauntered out of the room, leaving her suitcase sitting on the floor.

Glen frowned but picked up the suitcase and followed. "I made reservations at the Silver Moon," he called after her.

Tara made no comment until she reached the bottom step. Then she turned and glared up at him. "I don't think you should go to the Silver Moon."

"Why not?"

"That place is too expensive!"

He smiled in response. "I'm sure I can scrape together enough money to pay for two dinners."

"How do you even know Sinda likes Chinese food?"

"She said so. What's this sudden concern about restaurant prices?" Glen exhaled a puff of frustration. He was not in the mood for this conversation.

She shrugged.

Glen bent down and planted a kiss on her forehead. "I'll watch you cross the street." He paused a moment. "Oh, and Tara?"

"Yeah, Dad?"

"You'd better behave yourself tonight."

She pursed her lips. "Don't I always?"

WANDA E. BRUNSTETTER lives in Central Washington with her husband who is a pastor. She has two grown children and six grandchildren. Her hobbies include doll repairing, sewing, ventriloquism, stamping, reading, and gardening. Wanda and her husband have a puppet ministry, which they often share at other churches, Bible camps, and Bible schools. Wanda invites you to visit her website: http://hometown.aol.com/Wbrunstetter/index.html

Books by Wanda E. Brunstetter

HEARTSONG PRESENTS
HP254—A Merry Heart
HP421—Looking for a Miracle
HP465—Talking for Two
HP478—Plain and Fancy
HP486—The Hope Chest

The Neighborly Thing

Wanda E. Brunstetter

Heartsong Presents

In loving memory of my father,
William E. Cumby,
who helped me with the legalities of
opening my first doll hospital.

A note from the author:
I love to hear from my readers! You may correspond with me
by writing:

Wanda E. Brunstetter
Author Relations
PO Box 719
Uhrichsville, OH 44683

ISBN 1-58660-680-8

THE NEIGHBORLY THING

PRINTED IN THE U.S.A.

one

"The perfect home," Sinda Shull murmured as she stood on the sagging front porch of her new house. "Perfect for my needs, but oh, what a dump!"

Her friend, Carol Riggins, drew Sinda close for a hug. "Seattle's loss is Elmwood's gain, and now the town won't be the same." She snickered, then her expression sobered. "I'm really glad you decided to leave the past behind and move to Oregon for a fresh start."

Sinda's thoughts fluttered toward the past, then quickly shut down. That was part of her life better left uninvited. She pulled away from her friend, choosing not to comment on her reasons for moving from Seattle, Washington. "Sure hope I can figure out some way to turn this monstrosity into a real home."

"I thought you bought the place to use for your business."

"I did, but I have to live here too."

Carol nodded. "True, and fixing it up should help get your mind off the past."

Pushing back a strand of hair that had escaped her ponytail, Sinda frowned. Carol might think she knew all about Sinda's past, but the truth was, her friend knew very little about what had transpired in the Shull home over the years. When the Rigginses moved into their north Seattle neighborhood, Sinda and Carol were both twelve. By then Sinda and her father had already been living alone for two years. Dad didn't like her to have friends over, so Sinda usually played at Carol's house. It was probably better that way. . .less chance of Carol finding out her secrets.

Sinda heard footsteps and glanced to the left. A tall man wearing a mail carrier's uniform was walking up the sidewalk leading to the house next door. The sight of him pulled Sinda's mind back to the present, and she slapped at the dirt on her blue jeans. "Let's not spoil our day by talking about the past, okay?"

Carol pulled her fingers through her short blond curls and nodded. "We've managed to get you pretty well moved in with no problems, so I'd better get going before I ruin everything by dredging up old memories." She patted Sinda's arm. "I can't imagine what it must feel like to lose a parent, let alone both of them."

The image of her father and his recent death from a heart attack burned deep into Sinda's soul. In order to force the painful memories into submission, Sinda had to swallow hard and refocus her thoughts. "I–I appreciate all you've done today, Carol."

"What are friends for?" Carol gave Sinda another hug, then she turned to go. "Give a holler if you need my help with anything else," she called over her shoulder.

Sinda grimaced. "With the way this place looks, you can probably count on it."

ఌ

Glen Olsen poured himself a tall glass of milk, then another one for his ten-year-old daughter, Tara. It had been a long day, and he was bone tired. He'd encountered two new dogs on his route, been chewed out by an irate woman whose disability check hadn't arrived on time, and he had a blister the size of a silver dollar on his left foot. All Glen wanted to do was sit down, kick off his boots, and try to unwind before he had to fix supper.

He handed Tara her glass of milk and placed a jar of ginger cookies they'd baked the day before in the center of the kitchen table. "Have a seat and let's have a snack."

"Dad, have you met our new next-door neighbors yet?" Tara reached into the container and grabbed two cookies, which she promptly stuffed into her mouth.

Glen followed suit and washed his cookies down with a gulp of milk. "Nope, but when I got home this afternoon, I saw two women standing on the front porch."

Tara's brown eyes brightened. "Really? What were they doing?"

Glen dropped into the chair across from her and bent over to unlace his boots. "They were talking, Nosey Rosey."

"Dad!" Tara wrinkled her freckled nose and looked at him as though he'd lost his mind. "Did you see any kids my age?"

He gingerly slipped his left foot free and wiggled his toes. "Like I said. . .just the two women. I saw one of them drive off in a red sports car, and the other lady probably went inside."

Tara tapped her fingernails along the checkered tablecloth. "That's doesn't tell me much. When it comes to detective work, you're definitely not one of the top ten."

Glen chuckled. "What do you mean? I told you all I know. Just because I'm not as good at neighborhood snooping as some people I know. . ."

"I'm not a snoop! The correct word for my career is 'detective'!"

"Detective—snoop—what's the difference?" Glen wagged his finger. "You need to mind your own business, young lady. People don't like it when you spy on them."

"What makes you think I've been spying on the neighbors?"

"Elementary, my dear daughter. Elementary." Glen gulped down the rest of his milk and grabbed a napkin out of the wicker basket on the table. "May I remind you that you've done it before? I'm surprised you don't have the full history on our new neighbors by now."

Tara's mahogany eyes, so like her mother's, seemed to be challenging him, but surprisingly, she took their conversation in another direction. "These cookies are great, Dad. You're probably the best cook in the entire world!"

Glen raised his eyebrows. "I might be the best cook in our neighborhood, or maybe even the whole town of Elmwood, but certainly not the entire world. Besides, you usually help me with the cooking." He reached across the table and gave Tara's hand a gentle squeeze.

She smiled in response, revealing a pair of perfectly matched dimples. "Say, I've got a terrific idea!"

"Oh, no!" Glen slapped one hand against the side of his head. "Should I call out the Coast Guard, or does that come later?"

"Quit teasing, Dad."

"Okay, okay. What's your terrific idea, Kiddo?"

Tara's eyes lit up like a sunbeam as a slow smile swept across her face. "I think we should take some of these yummy cookies over there." Tara marched over to the cupboard and brought a heavy paper plate to the table, then piled it high with cookies.

Glen reached down to rub his sore foot and asked absently, "Over where?"

She smacked her hand against the table, and a couple cookies flew off the plate. "Over to our new neighbor's house. You're always lecturing me about being kind to our neighbors, so I thought it would be the neighborly thing to do."

"Let me get this straight," Glen said, reaching for one of the cookies that had fallen to the table. "You want to take some of our delicious, best-in-the-whole-neighborhood cookies, and go over to meet our new neighbors. Is that right?"

Tara jumped to her feet. "Exactly! That way we can find out if they have any kids my age." She tipped her head to one side. "Of course, if you're too scared—"

"Me? Scared? Now what would I have to be scared of?"

"That big old house is pretty creepy looking."

"For you, maybe," Glen said with a hearty laugh. "As for me—I'm not only a great cook, but I'm also a fearless warrior."

"Can we go now, Dad?"

Glen studied his daughter intently. It was obvious from the determined tilt of her chin that she was completely serious about this. Whenever Tara came up with one of her bright ideas, he knew she wasn't about to let it drop until he either agreed or laid down the law. In this case he thought her plan had merit. "I suppose your idea does beat spying over the garden fence," he said, sucking in his bottom lip in order to hold back the laughter that threatened to bubble over.

"I don't spy," she retorted as her hands went to her hips.

"I've heard through the grapevine that you're always spying on someone with those binoculars I made the mistake of buying you last Christmas. If you had your way, you'd probably be going over every square inch of our new neighbor's house with a fine-tooth comb." Glen waved his hand for emphasis.

"I would not!" Tara went back to the cupboard, took out some plastic wrap, and covered the plate of cookies. "Ready?"

Glen stood up. "I'm game if you are." He grabbed a light jacket from the coat tree near the back door, stepped into his slippers, and threw Tara her sweater. "Come on. I'll show you how brave I can be."

Glen glanced over his shoulder and saw that Tara was following his lead out the back door. As they stepped off the porch, he felt her jab him in the ribs. "Just in case you do get scared, remember that I'll be with you, Dad."

A catchy comeback flitted through Glen's mind, but he decided against saying anything more.

They moved across the grass, and Glen opened the high gate that separated their backyard from the neighbor's. The dilapidated, three-story home was in sharp contrast to the rest of the houses in their neighborhood. Dark, ragged-looking curtains hung at the windows, peeling green paint made the siding resemble alligator skin, and a sagging back porch indicated the whole house was desperately in need of an overhaul. The yard was equally run-down; the flowerbeds were filled with choking weeds, and the grass was so tall it looked like it hadn't been mowed for at least a year.

"This place gives me the creeps," Tara whispered as she knocked on the wooden edge of the rickety screen door. "I don't know why anyone would buy such a dump."

Glen shrugged. "It's not so bad, really. Nothing a few coats of paint and a little elbow grease wouldn't cure."

"Yeah, right," Tara muttered.

When the back door opened, a woman who appeared to be in her thirties stood before them holding a small vinyl doll in one hand. She was dressed in a pair of faded blue jeans and a bright orange sweatshirt smudged with dirt. Her long auburn hair was in a ponytail, and iridescent green eyes, peeking out of long eyelashes, revealed her obvious surprise. "May I help you?" she asked, quickly placing the doll on one end of the kitchen counter.

With a casualness he didn't feel, Glen leaned against the porch railing and offered the woman what he hoped was a pleasant smile. He cleared his throat a few times, wondering why it suddenly felt so dry. "My name's Glen Olsen, and this is my daughter, Tara. We're your next-door neighbors. We dropped by to welcome you to the neighborhood."

Tara held out the paper plate. "And to give you these."

The woman smiled slightly and took the offered cookies. "I'd invite you in, but the place is a mess right now." She fidgeted, and her gaze kept darting back and forth between Glen and Tara, making him wonder if she felt as nervous about meeting them as he did her.

"That's all right, Mrs.—"

"My name's Sinda Shull, and I'm not married," she said with a definite edge to her voice.

"I guess that means you don't have any kids," Tara interjected.

Glen gave his daughter a warning nudge, but before she could say anything more, the woman answered, "I have no children."

"But what about the—"

"We'd better get going," Glen said, cutting Tara off in mid-sentence. "Miss Shull is probably trying to get unpacked and settled in." His fingers twitched as he struggled with an unexplained urge to reach out and brush a wayward strand of tawny hair away from Sinda's face. Shifting his weight from one foot to the other, he quickly rubbed his sweaty palm against his jacket pocket and extended his hand. "It was nice meeting you."

As they shook, Glen noticed how small her hand was

compared to his. And it was ice cold. *She really must be nervous.* He moistened his lips, then smiled. "If you need anything, please let me know."

She let go and took a step backward. "Thanks, but I'm sure I won't need anything."

Glen felt a tug on his jacket sleeve. "Come on, Dad. Let's go home."

"Sure. Okay." He nodded at Sinda Shull. "Good night, then."

❧

Sinda didn't usually allow self-pity to take control of her thoughts, but tonight she couldn't seem to help herself. She'd only been living in Elmwood, Oregon, one day, and already she missed home—and yes, even Dad. In spite of her father's possessive, controlling, and sometimes harsh ways, until his death he'd been her whole world. He'd taken her to church, supplied food for the table, and put clothes on their backs. He had taught Sinda respect, obedience, and. . .

Sinda moved away from the kitchen table, placing her supper dishes in the sink. She was doing it again. . .thinking about the past. Dad was dead now, and for the first time in her life she was on her own. For the last year she'd learned to become independent, so what difference did her past make now? She blinked back tears and clenched her teeth. "I won't dwell on the things I can't change."

As she turned toward the cupboard, Sinda spotted the plate of cookies lying next to the doll she'd put there earlier. "Why was I so rude to the neighbors?" she moaned. "I don't think I even thanked them for the goodies."

She squeezed her eyes shut as a mental picture of her father flashed onto the screen of her mind. *How would Dad have reacted if he'd witnessed me being rude?* She took a deep breath, holding her sides for several seconds and willing the pain to go away. There was no point wasting time on these reflections, and there was no time for neighborly things. She had a house that would take a lot of work to make it livable, much less serve as a place of business. So what if she'd been rude to Glen Olsen and his little girl? They'd be living their lives, and she'd be living hers. If they never spoke again, what would it matter?

Sinda ran warm water into the sink and added some liquid detergent, staring at the tiny bubbles as they floated toward the plaster ceiling. "I came here to get away from the past, and I've got a job to do. So that's that!"

❧

"Our new neighbor seems kind of weird, doesn't she, Dad?" Tara asked as the two of them were finishing their supper of macaroni and cheese.

Glen had other thoughts on his mind, and even though he'd heard her question, he chose not to answer.

"Dad!"

He looked up from his half-eaten plate of food. "Yes, Tara?"

"Don't you think Sinda Shull is weird? Did you see the way she was dressed?"

Glen lifted his fork but didn't take a bite. "What's wrong with the way she was dressed? She just moved in, and those were obviously her working clothes."

Tara gazed at the ceiling. "She looked like a pumpkin in that goofy orange sweatshirt, and—"

"Do I need to remind you what the Bible says about loving our neighbors and judging others?" he interrupted. "The woman seemed nice enough to me, and it's not our place to pass judgment, even if she should turn out to be not so nice."

Tara groaned. "You would say that. You always try to look for the good in others."

"That's exactly what God wants us to do." Glen shoveled some macaroni into his mouth, then washed it down with a gulp of water.

She frowned at him. "What if the person you think is good turns out to be rotten to the core?"

"I hardly think Sinda Shull is rotten to the core." Glen shook his head. "Besides, only God knows what's in some-one's heart."

Tara wrinkled her nose. "You can believe whatever you like, but I've got a bad feeling about that woman. I'm trusting my instincts on this one."

"I say your instincts are way off!" He scowled. "And don't go getting any ridiculous notions about spying on Miss Shull. It's not the—"

"I know, I know," she interrupted. "It's not the neighborly thing to do."

He nodded.

Tara tapped a fingernail against her chin. "Can I ask you a question?"

"I suppose."

"Why would a woman who isn't married and has no kids be holding a doll when she answered the door?"

Glen shrugged. "Maybe she has relatives or friends with children."

Tara remained silent for several seconds, as though she were in deep thought. "She acted kind of nervous, didn't you think? And did you see those green eyes of hers?"

Glen smiled. Oh, he'd seen them all right. Even for the few minutes they'd been standing on Sinda's back porch, it had been hard to keep from staring into those pools of liquid emerald. *Get a grip,* he scolded himself. *You can't let some new neighbor woman make you start acting like a high school kid—especially not in front of your impressionable young daughter.*

"Sinda's eyes remind me of Jake," Tara said, jolting Glen out of his musings.

"Jake? What are you talking about, Tara?"

"She's got cat's eyes. She could probably hypnotize someone with those weird eyes."

Glen leaned on the table, casting a frown at his daughter. "I think you, Little Miss Detective, have an overactive imagination. You watch way too much TV, and I plan to speak to Mrs. Mayer about it. While I'm at work, she needs to watch you a bit more closely."

Tara's lower lip protruded. "I don't watch too much TV. I just have a sixth sense about people. Right now my senses are telling me that Sinda Shull is one weird lady, and she needs to be watched!"

two

Sinda pulled her white minivan into the driveway and stopped in front of the basement door. She had more than enough work to do today. There were boxes to unload, stacks of paperwork to go through, and numerous phone calls to make. The list seemed endless, and there was no telling how long it might take to get everything accomplished.

With mustered enthusiasm, Sinda climbed out of the van and went around to open the tailgate. There were five large boxes in back. Knowing they wouldn't unload themselves, she pulled the first one toward her and began to carefully lift it.

"Hi, there!"

Sinda startled at the sound of a child's voice. The same little girl who had brought her cookies the other night was crouched in the picture-perfect flower bed next door. She had a shovel in one of her gloved hands and appeared to be weeding.

"Were you speaking to me?" Sinda asked from across the small white picket fence.

"I said 'hi.' " The child stood up and brushed a clump of dirt from the knees of her dark blue overalls.

"Hello. It's Tara, right?"

The young girl wore her cinnamon brown hair in a pony-tail, and it bounced with each step she took toward Sinda. "Yeah, my name's Tara." She pressed her body against the fence, and her dark eyes looked at Sinda with such intensity it made her feel like she was on trial.

Sinda glanced down at her blue cutoffs and yellow T-shirt, gave her ponytail a self-conscious flip with one hand, then lifted the box. "I guess we're both doing chores today, Tara."

Tara pushed a loose strand of hair away from her face. "Would you like me to see if Dad can come over and carry

15

some of those boxes into the house? The one you're holding looks kind of heavy."

Sinda clutched the box tightly to her chest. She hated to admit it, but it was a bit weighty. Accepting help from a neighbor she hardly knew was not her style, though. It hadn't been Dad's style either. In fact, if he'd had his way, she wouldn't have associated with any of their Seattle neighbors during her adolescence. It was lucky for Sinda that she and Carol had gone to school together. That's when they'd become good friends, and Sinda had decided to play at Carol's house as often as she could. Of course, it was usually after school, when Dad was still at work, or on a Saturday, when he was busy running errands.

"You look really tired. Should I call Dad or what?"

Tara's persistence jolted Sinda out of her musings. "No, I'm fine. Don't trouble your father."

"I'm sure it wouldn't be any trouble. Dad likes to help people in need."

Sinda grunted. "What makes you think I'm in need?"

Tara moved quickly away from the fence, looking as though she'd been stung by a wasp. "Okay, whatever."

"I'm sorry I snapped," Sinda called as she started up the driveway toward her basement entrance. "Thanks for the offer of help."

Tara went back to her weeding, but Sinda had an inkling she hadn't seen or heard the last of the extroverted child.

A short time later, when she'd finished unloading the back of the van, Sinda went around front and opened the passenger door. She blew the dust off her watch and checked the time, then withdrew a large wicker basket and carried it into the house. "How I wish this was the last load," she muttered, "but I'll probably be hauling boxes from my storage unit for weeks."

❧

"Just what do you think you're doing, young lady?" Glen barked when he entered Tara's bedroom and found her gazing out the window with binoculars pointing at the front yard of their new neighbor's house.

Tara jumped, nearly dropping the binoculars. "Dad! Don't scare me like that!"

"Sorry, but I did knock first. You obviously didn't hear me, because you were too busy spying."

"I was watching Sinda Shull." Tara turned away from the window. "I don't trust her. I think she's up to something."

Glen planted both hands on his hips. "Up to something? What do you think the woman's up to?"

Tara dropped the binoculars onto the bed and moved closer to Glen. She spoke in a hushed tone, as though they might be overheard. "I don't think I have quite enough evidence yet, but with a little more time, maybe I can get something incriminating on her."

He raised his eyebrows. *Where does this kid learn such big words?* "Honestly, Tara. What kind of incriminating evidence could you possibly have on someone as nice as Sinda Shull?"

Tara flopped onto the bed with a groan. "Nice? How do you know she's nice? You don't even know her."

Glen reached up to rub the back of his neck. He was beginning to feel a headache coming on, and he sure didn't need an argument with his mischievous daughter right now. "Sinda seemed nice enough to me."

"You've only met her once," Tara argued. "If you knew her better, you'd soon see that my intuition is right."

Glen's lips curved into a smile. "You know, Kiddo, you might be right about that."

"You think she's up to something?"

He shook his head. "No, but I think we should get to know her better."

"Oh. I guess that would help."

"In fact, I believe I'll invite her over here for dinner. Tomorrow afternoon sounds good to me."

Tara's expression turned to sheer panic. "You're kidding, right?"

"I'm totally serious. What better way to get acquainted than over a nice candlelit dinner?"

"Candlelit?" Tara came straight off the bed. "Don't you think that might be carrying neighborliness a bit too far?" She sniffed deeply. "Besides, Sunday is our day to be together. We don't want to spoil it by having some stranger around, do we?"

Glen bent down, so his eyes were level with Tara's. "You said you thought it would help if we got better acquainted with the neighbor."

"I know, but—"

"Then don't throw cold water on my plans. I think I should go over there right now and ask her. If Sinda agrees to join us for dinner, I'll fix fried chicken, and maybe some of those flaky buttermilk biscuits you like so well." He clasped his hands together and flexed his fingers until several of them popped. "Let's see. . .what shall we have for dessert?"

Tara grabbed his arm and gave it a firm shake. "Dad, get a grip! It's just one little dinner, so we can find out more about the weirdo neighbor. You don't have to make such a big deal out of it."

"No more 'weird neighbor' comments. In the book of Luke we are told to love our neighbors as ourselves, and Romans 10:13 reminds us that love does no harm to its neighbor. That includes not making unkind comments about our neighbors." He started for the door, but hesitated. "I'm going over to Sinda's, and when I get back, you should be doing something constructive. And put those binoculars away."

"Can I borrow the camcorder for awhile?"

"No."

"But, Dad, I—"

"You've done enough spying for one day."

略

The back door of Sinda's house hung wide open, with only the rickety old screen door to offer protection from the cool spring breeze whistling under the porch eaves. Glen's feet brought him to the door as his thoughts wandered. *Is this really a good idea? Will Sinda be receptive to my dinner invitation?* With a resolve to go through with the plan, he looked around for a doorbell but found none. He rapped lightly on the side of the screen door, and when there was no response, he called out, "Hello! Anybody home?" Still nothing. He leaned forward and peered through a hole in the screen, listening for any sounds that might be coming from within. "Hello!"

There were no lights on in the kitchen, and he couldn't see much past the table and chairs sitting near the door. The thought crossed his mind to see if the screen was unlocked, and if it wasn't, maybe he'd poke his head inside. *That would be categorized as snooping,* he reminded himself. *I'm getting as bad as that would-be detective daughter of mine.*

Glen had about decided to give up when another thought popped into his mind. *Maybe Sinda's out front. That's where Tara was spying on her.*

He stepped off the back porch, nearly tripping on one of the loose boards, then started around the side of the house. He had just rounded the corner when he ran straight into Sinda. She held a bulky cardboard box in her arms and appeared to be heading for the front door.

"Excuse me!" the two said in unison, each taking a step backward.

"That box looks kind of heavy. Would you like me to carry it for you?" Glen offered.

She shook her head. "It's not that heavy. Besides, I've already made several trips to my storage unit today, and I can manage fine on my own."

Glen eyed her speculatively. Tara was right about one thing. Sinda's green eyes did look sort of catlike. It was difficult not to stare at them. He drew from his inner reserve and lowered his gaze. *Get yourself under control. You didn't come over here to ask for a date or anything. It's just a simple home-cooked meal, done purely as a neighborly gesture.*

Glen cleared his throat a few times, and Sinda gave him a questioning look. "Is there something I can do for you, Mr. Olsen?"

"Glen. Please call me Glen." Now that he'd found his voice again, he decided to plunge ahead. "I was wondering—that is, my daughter and I would like to invite you over for dinner tomorrow afternoon." He rushed on. "I make some pretty tasty fried chicken, and there's always plenty. Please say you'll come."

Sinda shifted the box in her arms. He could tell it was much too heavy for her, but if she didn't want his help, what could he do about it?

"I wouldn't want to put you or your wife out any," Sinda stated as she moved toward the house.

Glen followed. "My wife?"

She nodded but kept on walking.

"Oh, I'm not married. I mean, I was married, but my wife died of leukemia when Tara was a year old."

Sinda stopped in her tracks and turned to face him. Her green eyes had darkened, and if he wasn't mistaken, a few tears were gathering in the corners of those gorgeous orbs.

"I'm so sorry, Mr. Olsen. . .I mean, Glen. I'm sure it must be difficult for you to be raising a daughter all alone."

"It can be challenging at times," he admitted.

"I'm surprised you haven't remarried," Sinda remarked. "A child really does need a mother, you know."

An odd statement coming from a single lady, and her tone sounded almost reprimanding. Glen shrugged. "Guess I've never found a woman who could put up with me." *Or my daughter,* he added mentally. The truth was, he had dated a few women over the years, but Tara always managed to scare them off. She was more than a little possessive of him and had made his dates feel uncomfortable with her unfriendly attitude and constant interrogations. Most of them backed away before he could deal with Tara's jealousy.

"How 'bout it?" Glen asked, returning to the question at hand. "Will you come for dinner? It'll give us a chance to get better acquainted."

"Fried chicken does sound rather tasty." Sinda paused and

flicked her tongue across her lower lip. "Okay, I'll come."

Glen could hardly believe she had accepted his invitation. The other night Sinda seemed rather standoffish. Maybe she'd just been tired. "How does one o'clock sound?" he asked.

"That'll be fine. Can I bring anything?"

"Just a hearty appetite." He turned toward his own yard. "See you tomorrow, Sinda."

three

"I still don't see why we've gotta have that woman over for dinner," Tara whined as Glen drove them home from church Sunday afternoon.

"You're the one who gave me the idea of getting to know her better." He smiled. "Who knows, you might even find you'll actually enjoy yourself."

"I doubt it," Tara mumbled.

"Just try," he said through clenched teeth. "Oh, and Tara?"

"Yeah, Dad?"

"Be on your best behavior today. No prying into Sinda's private life. If she volunteers any information about herself, that's one thing, but I don't want you bombarding her with a bunch of silly questions. Is that clear?" He glanced at her out of the corner of his eye.

She shrugged. "How are we gonna find out what she's up to in that creepy old house if we don't ask a few questions?"

Glen's patience was waning, and he scowled at Tara. "Sinda is not up to anything."

"I saw her carrying a wicker basket into her house the other day," she persisted. "And you know what I heard?"

"There's nothing unusual about a wicker basket."

"But I know I heard a—"

"Tara Mae Olsen!" Glen usually had more patience with his daughter, but today she was pushing too far. "I don't want to hear another word. Sinda Shull is our neighbor, and we're going to enjoy dinner while we try to get to know her better."

Tara sniffed deeply. "I'm just glad you didn't ask her to go to church with us."

A pair of amazing green eyes flashed into Glen's mind, and he smiled. "I should have thought of that. Maybe next time I will ask her. If she hasn't already found a church home, that is."

ع

Sinda glanced at her reflection in the bay window as she stood on the front porch of the neighbor's split-level rambler. She'd decided to wear a pair of khaki slacks and an off-white knit top for dinner at the Olsens'. She'd chosen a pair of amber-colored tortoise shell combs to hold her hair away from her face, and even though she might look presentable, she felt like a fish out of water. *Probably as out of place as my archaic house looks next to this modern one,* she mused. *What on earth possessed me to accept Glen's dinner invitation?* It wasn't like her to be sociable with people she barely knew. Dad had taught her to be wary of strangers and not to let anyone know much about their personal business.

With that thought in mind, Sinda was on the verge of turning for home, but the front door unexpectedly swung open. "You're ten minutes late," Tara grumbled as she motioned Sinda inside.

Sinda studied the child a few seconds. A thick mane of brown hair fell freely down Tara's back, and she was dressed in a red jumper with a white blouse. The freckles dotting the girl's nose made her look like a cute little pixie, even if she did seem to have a chip on both shoulders. *Such a rude young lady. Why, if I'd talked to someone like that when I was a child. . .*

With determination, Sinda refocused her thoughts. "I'm sorry about being late. I hope I haven't ruined dinner."

"It would take more than ten minutes to wreck one of Dad's great meals. He's the best cook in the whole state of Oregon."

"Then I guess I'm in for a treat," Sinda responded with a forced smile.

"Dad's out in the kitchen getting everything served up. He said for us to go into the dining room."

Sinda followed Tara down the hall and into a cozy but formal eating area. It was tastefully decorated, with a large oak table and six matching chairs occupying the center of the room. The walls were painted off-white, with a border of pale pink roses running along the top. A small pot of purple pansies sat in the middle of the table with two pink taper candles on either side. The atmosphere was soft and subtle. Hardly something most men would have a hand in, Sinda noted. She offered Tara another guarded smile. "The flowers are lovely."

"They're from my mother's garden. She planted lots of flowers the year before I was born. Dad takes good care of them, so they keep coming back every year. He says as long as the flowers are alive, we'll have a part of Mom with us." Tara lifted her chin and stared at Sinda with a look of defiance. "Dad loved her a lot."

"I'm sure he did." Sinda swallowed against the constriction she felt tightening her throat. She had to blink several times to keep unwanted tears from spilling over. *What's wrong with me today? I should be able to get through a simple thing like dinner at the neighbor's without turning into a basket case.*

"Have a seat," Tara said. "I'll go tell Dad you're here."

The young girl sashayed out of the room, and Sinda pulled out a chair and sat down. Tara returned a few minutes later, carrying a glass pitcher full of ice water. She filled the three glasses, placed the pitcher on the table, then flopped into the seat directly across from Sinda.

"Something smells good," Sinda murmured, for lack of anything better to say. Why was Tara staring at her like that? It made her feel like a bug under a microscope.

"That would be Dad's fried chicken. He wanted me to tell you that he'll be right in." Tara plunked her elbows on the table, rested her chin in her palms, and continued to stare.

"Is there something I can do to help?" Sinda asked hopefully.

"Nope. Dad's got everything under control."

"What grade are you in?" Sinda was hoping a change in subject might ease some of the tension.

Tara began playing with the napkin beside her plate. She folded it in several different directions, opened it, and then refolded it. "I'm in the fourth grade," she finally answered without looking up from her strange-looking work of art.

"Do you like school?"

"It's okay, but I can't wait for summer break in June. Dad and I always do lots of fun stuff in the summer time. We usually spend all our Sundays together too." Tara looked pointedly at Sinda.

Refusing to let the child intimidate her, Sinda asked, "Who looks out for you when your father's at work?"

"Mrs. Mayer. She's been my baby-sitter ever since I can remember."

"Is your dad a mailman?" Sinda asked, taking the conversation in another direction. "I've seen him dressed in a uniform, and it looked like the kind mail carriers usually wear."

Tara nodded. "Yep, he's a mailman all right. Dad has a walking route on the other side of town."

No wonder he looks so physically fit. Sinda had noticed a whole lot more about Glen Olsen than the uniform he wore, but she'd never have admitted it—especially not to his daughter.

"Now that you know everything about us, tell me something about you," Tara blurted out.

Sinda felt her face flush. She wasn't about to disclose anything from her past. Her life was not a book, left open for anyone to read. "There—isn't much to tell."

"Why did you buy that creepy old house?"

Sinda gave Tara a blank stare. Where were the child's manners, anyway?

"I heard that all the property on this block belonged to the first owner of your house. They built new homes all around it." Tara wrinkled her nose, as though a putrid smell had suddenly invaded the room. "Your house looks really weird sitting on the same block with a bunch of nice homes."

How could Sinda argue with that? Especially when she'd thought the same thing herself. "You're probably right," she agreed. "However, I got the house for a reasonable price, and it's perfect for my needs."

Tara's eyes brightened as she leaned forward on her elbows. "What exactly are those needs?"

Sinda blinked rapidly. *Why is she asking so many questions?*

"What do you do in that big old house?"

"Do?"

"Yeah. What I really want to know is why you—"

Tara's words were cut off when her father stepped through the swinging door separating the kitchen from the dining room. "Sorry to keep you lovely ladies waiting. It took some time to get everything dished up." Glen looked over at Sinda and offered her a friendly grin. "I hope you'll soon see—or rather, taste that the wait was worth it." He placed a huge platter of fried chicken on the table. "I'm glad you could join us today, Sinda."

"It was nice of you to invite me, Glen."

Glen took a seat at the head of the table. "Tara, would you please run out to the kitchen and bring in the salad and potatoes?"

"Can't you do it?"

Sinda sucked in her breath, waiting to see how Glen would respond to his daughter's sassy remark.

"I'll be lighting the candles," he said patiently.

Sinda could hardly believe how soft-spoken he was. She'd expected him to shout at Tara and tell her she was being insolent.

"Dad, you're really not going to turn this into a fancy dinner, are you?" Tara asked, casting her father a pleading glance.

Glen turned toward Sinda and gave her a quick wink. "It isn't every day that the Olsens get to entertain someone so charming."

Sinda felt the heat of embarrassment creep up the back of her neck. There was no denying it—Glen was quite a handsome man. His wavy, dark hair and sparkling blue eyes were enough to turn any woman's head. She averted his gaze by pretending to study the floral pattern on the dinner plate in front of her.

"Tara, I asked you to bring in the salad and potatoes."

"Okay, okay. . .I'm going."

Tara left the room, and Glen pulled a book of matches from the front pocket of his pale blue dress shirt. He proceeded to light the candles and had just finished when Tara returned, carrying a bowl of mashed potatoes.

"Don't forget the salad," he reminded.

The child gave him a disgruntled look, then she stomped off toward the kitchen. A few minutes later she was back with a tossed green salad.

"Thank you, Tara. Great, we're all set now," Glen said, offering Sinda another warm smile. She was beginning to wonder if he ever quit smiling. Even when his daughter was acting like a brat, he kept a pleasant look on his face. It was a little disconcerting.

Tara reached for a piece of chicken, but Glen stopped her. "We haven't prayed yet."

"Sorry. I forgot."

When Glen and Tara bowed their heads, Sinda did the same. It had been awhile since she'd prayed—even for a meal. She knew why she'd given up praying; she just wasn't sure exactly when it had happened. Somehow it felt right to pray today, though. Glen seemed so earnest in his praises to God. Of course. . .

"Amen."

When she realized the blessing was over, Sinda opened her eyes and helped herself to a drumstick. "Everything looks and smells wonderful." She bit into the succulent meat and wasn't disappointed.

Tara sniffed the air. "Speaking of smells—I think something's burning."

Glen jumped up, nearly knocking over his glass of water. "My buttermilk biscuits!" He raced from the room, leaving Sinda alone with his daughter one more time.

Sinda spooned some mashed potatoes onto her plate and added a pat of butter from the butter dish sitting near her. She was about to take a bite, when the next question came.

"Do you know who Mrs. Higgins was?"

"My Realtor said she was the previous owner of my house."

"Yep, and she was really weird too."

Sinda wasn't sure if Tara had emphasized the word *she* on purpose or not, but with a slight shrug, she decided to ignore the remark.

"Mrs. Higgins hardly ever left that creepy old house, and sometimes you could hear strange noises coming from over there." Tara's forehead wrinkled. "Some of the neighborhood kids think your house is haunted."

"What do you believe, Tara?"

"Dad says the noises were probably her old blind dog, howlin' at the moon. He thinks I shouldn't believe what other kids say—especially stuff like that." The child tore a piece of dark meat from the chicken leg she'd speared with her fork. "You couldn't pay me enough money to live in that creepy old place." She tapped the tines of her fork against the edge of her plate.

Glen stepped back into the dining room, interrupting Tara a second time. "That was close! My biscuits were just seconds from being ruined." He set the basket of rolls and a jar of strawberry jam on the table, then took his seat. "I believe I can finally join you in eating this meal."

"The fried chicken is wonderful," Sinda said, licking her lips. "I think Tara's right. You are the best cook in Oregon."

Glen transmitted a smile that could have melted the ice cubes in Sinda's glass of water. "You'll have to try some of my famous barbecued chicken this summer."

"Oh, great," Tara muttered.

Glen shot his daughter a look that Sinda construed as a warning, and she swallowed so hard she nearly choked. Maybe Tara's dad wasn't quite as pleasant or patient as he first let on. "What did you say, Tara?" Glen's voice had raised at least an octave.

"I said, 'That sounds great.'"

Glen nodded at Tara, then Sinda. "I think so too."

Sinda dipped her head, unsure of what to think or how to respond.

"So, how about it, Sinda? Would you be interested in trying some of my barbecued chicken sometime this summer?"

Without even thinking, she replied, "I always enjoy a good barbecue." *Now, what made me say that?*

"Great!" Glen declared with another winning smile. "The first time I do barbecued chicken, I'll be sure to let you know."

four

Glen couldn't believe his eyes! Tara was peering through the cracks in the tall fence that separated their backyard from Sinda's. He'd just paid Mrs. Mayer her monthly check for watching Tara and seen her to her car. Now he had to deal with this? Slowly, he snuck up behind Tara and dropped one hand to her shoulder. "At it again, Miss Olsen?"

She spun around. "Dad! You've gotta quit sneakin' up on me like that. I'm too young to die of a heart attack."

"Maybe so, but you're not too young to be turned over my knee," he said, biting back a smile. While Glen did believe in discipline, he'd never had to resort to spanking Tara. Ever since she was old enough to sit in front of the TV, and he'd discovered how much she enjoyed it, he had used restrictions from television whenever she got out of line. It had always been fairly effective too.

With hands planted firmly on her small hips, Tara stared up at him. "Dad, I was only—"

"Don't say anything more," he interrupted. "I'm not interested in your excuses." He glanced down at the ground. "Look where you're standing! You're going to ruin your mother's flowers if you're not careful."

Tara hopped out of the flower bed, just missing the toe of his boot. "Sorry," she mumbled. "I'll try to be more careful when I'm doing my investigating."

"I think you should leave the detective work to the Elmwood Police Department and try acting your age, Tara— keeping in mind that you're only ten years old and should be playing, not spying." Glen pointed toward the house. "Why don't you go play with your dolls for awhile?"

Tara's forehead wrinkled. "I can't waste my time playing,

30

Dad. I'm on a case right now. Besides, dolls are dumb. I put mine away in the hall closet ages ago."

He drew in a deep breath, reached for Tara's hand, and led her to the picnic table on the other side of the yard. "Why don't we have some cookies and lemonade? After we've filled our stomachs with something sweet, maybe we can talk about this some more." He guided her to one of the wooden benches.

Tara's eyes brightened. "That's a great idea, Dad. Mrs. Mayer made fresh lemonade when I got home from school. I think there's still a few ginger cookies left too." She smiled up at him. "Of course, you're gonna have to make more pretty soon. Can't have an empty cookie jar, now can we?"

"No, that would never do," Glen said with a chuckle. "Maybe one evening this week I'll do some more baking, but that's only if you can stay out of trouble."

She offered him a sheepish grin. "I think I can manage."

"Good girl." Glen gave one of her braids a light tug. "Don't move from this spot. I'll be right back with cookies and lemonade."

When he returned a few minutes later, Glen was relieved to see that Tara was still sitting at the picnic table, and Jake was lying in her lap, purring like a motorboat.

"That cat sure has it easy," Glen said as he placed a tray loaded with cookies, napkins, a pitcher of lemonade, and two glasses in the center of the table. "All he ever does is laze around."

Tara stroked the gray and white cat behind its ears. "Yeah, he's got life made most of the time. Of course, he does work pretty hard when he chases down mice or poor, defenseless birds."

Glen took a seat on the bench across from her and studied the cat. "His green eyes sure are pretty."

Tara reached for a cookie. "Speaking of green eyes—I need to tell you something about our green-eyed neighbor lady."

Glen snapped to attention. "Sinda?" Against his will, and probably better judgment, he'd been thinking about Sinda ever since she'd come to dinner.

"Uh-huh."

"What about her?"

Tara leaned as far across the table as she could and whispered, "I saw her carrying more boxes into the house today."

"Sinda only moved in a few weeks ago, Tara. She told me the other day that she still has some things in storage and is bringing them home a little at a time."

"You don't understand," Tara asserted. "There was something really strange about one of those boxes."

Glen raised his eyebrows. "Strange? In what way?"

"Well, there was a—"

Tara's words were halted when Jake screeched, leaped off her lap, sailed across the yard, then scampered up the maple tree. Tara jumped up. "Ow! Stupid cat! He dug his claws into my legs!"

"I wonder what's gotten into him?" Glen shook his head. "It's not like Jake to carry on like that for no reason."

"That's why," Tara said, pointing to the gate that separated their backyard from Sinda's. It was open slightly, and a puny black dog poked its head through the opening. "Oh, great! You know how much Jake hates dogs."

A smile lifted the corners of Glen's mouth. "Yeah, and that little dog looks so ferocious."

Before Tara could respond, the dog took off like a streak of lightning, heading into the Olsens' yard, straight for the maple tree. Sinda was right behind him, calling, "Bad dog! Sparky, come back here right now!"

Glen's smile grew wider as he watched Sinda chase the small dog around his yard. He left the picnic table and moved toward her. "Is that your dog?"

"Yes," Sinda answered breathlessly. "He's a bundle of fury too! He won't come when I call him, and I've already discovered that he likes to sneak out of the yard. No wonder he was advertised as 'free to good home.'"

Sparky was now poised under the maple tree, barking

furiously and looking as though he could devour a mountain lion.

"He's after Jake!" Tara screamed, running toward the dog. "Dad, do something, quick!"

Sinda gave Glen a questioning look. "Jake?"

"Jake is Tara's cat. He ran up the tree when your pooch poked his head into our yard."

"I'm sorry," Sinda apologized. She moved in on Sparky, bent down, and scooped the yapping terrier into her arms.

"I didn't even know you owned a dog," Glen remarked. "We haven't seen or heard anything of him until a few minutes ago."

"Actually, I don't. I mean, I didn't have a dog before today." Sinda had to yell in order to be heard above the dog's frantic barking.

"He's kind of cute. Probably good company for you," Glen said in an equally loud voice.

"I did get him for companionship, but I also wanted a watchdog." Sinda held on tightly to the squirming, yapping terrier.

"He sure does bark loud. That should be enough to scare anyone off," Tara put in.

"Maybe he'll calm down if we move away from the tree." Glen took Sinda's arm and guided her toward the picnic table. "Would you like to join us for some cookies and lemonade? I'll go inside and get another glass."

Sinda looked down at the bundle of fur in her arms. "Thanks, but I'd better get this little rascal back home." She started moving toward the gate.

"Why do you need a watchdog?" Tara asked, stepping in front of Sinda. "Is there something weird going on in that creepy old house of yours?"

"Tara!"

"No, no. I mean, everything's fine," Sinda stammered.

Glen couldn't help but notice how flustered she was. Her face was red as a tomato, her hair was in complete disarray, and she looked like she was on the verge of tears. "Tara, move out of Sinda's way so she can take the dog back to her yard."

Tara stepped aside, but Glen could see by the stubborn set of her jaw that she was none too happy about it.

Sinda offered Glen the briefest of smiles, then she disappeared into her yard.

"What's that scowl you're wearing about?" Glen asked as Tara slumped onto the picnic table bench.

"Don't you see it, Dad?"

"See what?"

Tara squinted her eyes at him. "Can't you see how weird Sinda is?"

"I don't think she's weird." Glen snorted. "You, on the other hand, are apparently getting some weird ideas from watching too much TV. I'm going to speak to Mrs. Mayer about putting a limit on how much television you can watch after school."

"But, Dad, I—"

"A girl your age should be playing with her friends, not sitting in front of the TV all afternoon." Glen made an arch with his hand. "Instead, you're trying to dig up something on the neighbors!" He glanced across the yard searching for inspiration. "The flower beds could use some investigating. As soon as you finish your snack, you can get busy tending the garden."

Tara stuck out her lower lip and folded her arms across her chest. "I didn't do anything wrong."

Glen held up one finger. "You were spying." A second finger joined the first. "You were rude to Sinda." A third finger came up. "Then you said she's weird." He frowned deeply. "We keep discussing these same manners problems over and over, Tara. I'm going inside to start supper. You need to have that weeding finished before it's ready."

❧

By the time Sinda clipped a leash to Sparky's collar and secured him to a long chain hooked to the end of her clothesline, she was all done in. "Maybe getting a dog was a bad idea," she mumbled as she gave the furry creature a gentle pat. "So far, you've been nothing but trouble."

The little dog tipped his head and looked up at her as though he was truly sorry. Sinda couldn't help but smile. "I'll bring you inside after awhile." She turned and headed for the house. Sparky let out a pathetic whine, and she almost changed her mind about bringing him in before she fixed supper. When she was growing up, Sinda had always wanted a dog, but her father would never allow it. He used to say that pets were nothing but trouble, and after today Sinda thought he might have been right. Still, dogs were supposed to be companions and loyal friends. At least the mutts she'd seen on TV had been devoted to their masters.

When Sinda reached the back porch, she stopped beside the outside faucet and turned on the spigot. They hadn't had much rain yet this spring, and she figured the yard, though overgrown, could use a good drink. As the sprinkler came on, a spray of water shot into the air, and a miniature rainbow glistened through the mist.

She swallowed against the nodule that had formed in her throat. Rainbows always made Sinda think of her mother and, like it was only yesterday, she could hear Mother saying, "Rainbows are a reminder of God's promises. Whenever you see one, remember how much He loves you."

"Do You love me, God?" Sinda whispered as she looked up at the cloudless sky. "Has anyone ever truly loved me?"

The telephone was ringing when Sinda entered the kitchen a few minutes later. She grabbed the receiver with one hand while she reached for a towel with the other. In the process of turning on the hose, she'd managed to get her hand and both sneakers wet. Of course, when a faucet leaked like a sieve, what else could she expect?

"Hello," she said breathlessly into the cordless phone.

"Hi, Sinda, it's me."

Sinda dropped into a chair at the kitchen table. "Hey, Carol, how are you?"

"I was going to ask you the same question. I haven't heard

from you in awhile, and I was worried you might have worked yourself to death."

"Not quite, but from the looks of things, I'll be forever trying to get the rest of my things unpacked, not to mention getting this old place fixed up so it's livable."

"Know what I think you need?"

"What?"

"A break from all that work."

Sinda couldn't argue with that. She'd been working around the clock ever since she moved into the monstrosity she was dumb enough to call "home."

"How about meeting me for lunch at Elmwood City Park tomorrow afternoon? If you don't take a little break, you'll end up cranky as a bear who's lost all his hair."

"I guess I could spare an hour or so."

"Great! See you at one, and be ready for fun!"

Sinda grinned. Carol had always thought she was poet. Over the years, her friend's goofy rhymes and lighthearted banter had gotten Sinda through more than one pity party. *At least Carol taught me how to laugh.* Sinda wondered what her life would have been like if she'd been raised in a normal home with two loving parents. Instead, her childhood had been filled with loneliness, disappointment, countless rules, and sometimes hostility. But it was all Mother's fault. Dad went through so much because of her.

"Sinda, are you still there?"

Carol's question drove Sinda's thoughts back to the present, and she felt grateful. She was tired of living in the past. Tired of dwelling on the negative. She'd come to Elmwood to begin a new life, and she was determined to at least make her business venture successful.

"I'm here, Carol," she murmured. "I'll see you tomorrow at one."

five

"I'm glad you suggested this little outing," Sinda told Carol as they settled onto a park bench. She leaned back with a contented sigh. "It's such a beautiful spring day, and everything is so lush and green."

"It's that time of year, my dear." Carol needled Sinda in the ribs. "We usually get lots of liquid sunshine in the spring, but this year we're falling short of our average rainfall, so it won't stay green long if we don't get some rain soon."

Sinda made no comment, and Carol took their conversation in another direction. "You know, I was beginning to worry about you."

"How come?"

"Ever since you moved here, all you've done is work. It's been nearly a month, so I thought it was time you got out of that stuffy old house and did something fun."

Sinda opened her lunch sack and withdrew the ham sandwich she'd thrown together for their Saturday afternoon picnic. "For your information, I have gotten out of the house a few times."

"Really? Where did you go, Miss Social Butterfly?" Carol laughed and gave Sinda's arm a little squeeze.

"I've been shopping a few times, made several trips to my storage unit, stopped at the Department of Licensing, and I had dinner at the neighbor's one Sunday afternoon."

Carol raised her eyebrows. "Which neighbor was that?"

"The one next door. I'm sure I told you about Glen and his daughter bringing me some cookies the day I moved in."

"Yes, you did, but you didn't say anything about having dinner with them." Carol puckered her lips. "I'm surprised to hear you're seeing a man. You've never been much for dating."

37

"I'm not seeing anyone," Sinda said, choosing to ignore her friend's reminder about her lack of a social life. "It was just a friendly, get-to-know-your-neighbor dinner. Don't read any more into it than that."

Carol shook her head slowly. "I'm glad to have you living closer, but I'd be even happier if I knew you were truly at peace. You've had moods of melancholy as long as I've known you, and any time I've asked what's wrong, you've always avoided the subject."

"I appreciate your concern—always have, in fact. I've just never wanted to talk about my problems." Sinda stared off into space. "Besides, talking doesn't change anything."

"Maybe not, but it's good for the soul, which in turn brings happier thoughts," Carol responded.

Sinda glanced back at her friend. "My work keeps me plenty busy. And I have a good friend who meets me at the park for lunch whenever she thinks I'm working too much." She paused and winked at Carol. "That's all the happiness I need. Besides, you should concern yourself with your own love life and quit worrying about me."

Carol smiled and crossed her fingers. "I think I may have found my man."

"Is it the guy you told me about who works at the bank?"

"Gary Tarrol is our new loan officer." Carol elbowed Sinda in the ribs. "I don't know what I'll do if we should start dating and things get serious."

For a minute Sinda wondered if her friend was as leery of marriage as she was, but then she remembered how boy crazy Carol had been when they were teenagers. In fact, Sinda was amazed that Carol wasn't already married and raising a family.

"My motto is: Find the right guy and let your heart fly!" Carol continued. She batted her eyelashes dramatically. "Can you imagine me living the rest of my life with a name like Carol Tarrol?"

Sinda giggled. "It might be kind of cute. Especially since you like rhyming so well."

Her friend grimaced and opened her can of soda. "Not that well. Maybe I should look for someone with a better last name." She took a drink, then wiped her mouth on a napkin. "Now tell me—how's business?"

Sinda frowned. "I haven't done much advertising yet, so things are still kind of slow. There are lots of kids in this world, though, and just as many eager adults. I'm sure I'll do okay once the word gets out. In fact, I'll probably do as well here in Oregon as I did in the state of Washington."

"I have a friend who might need your services," Carol said. "She has a four-year-old daughter."

"Tell her to give me a call. I'm sure we can work something out." Sinda tossed her empty sandwich wrapper in the garbage and stood up. "Let's take a quick hike around the lake, then I need to get back home." As they started to walk away, she glanced over her shoulder. There were two young girls crouched in the bushes, not far from the bench where she and Carol had been sitting. One of the children wore her brown hair in pigtails. *That's Tara Olsen. Now, why would she be hiding in the bushes?*

❧

Sinda stood in front of her open kitchen window, talking on the phone. "Yes, they're quite safe in my basement. I'd be happy to take her off your hands," she said into the receiver. "We can discuss the price further once I've taken a good look at her." Sinda jotted a few notes on a tablet she kept near the phone, said good-bye, and hung up. Mrs. Kramer would be by soon with her delivery, then Sinda could grab a quick bite of dinner and try to get a few bills paid.

"Oh to be wealthy and carefree," she murmured. "Even carefree would be nice."

Sinda could feel a cord of tension grip her body, like a confining belt after a heavy meal. Her mouth compressed into a tight line as her mind drug her unwillingly back to the past. Dad had always stressed the importance of good stewardship. In his words that meant "Pay every bill on time, give God His ten percent, and never spend money foolishly." Sinda tried to be prompt about bill paying, but now that Dad was gone, she no longer worried about giving God any money. Why should she? God hadn't done much for her. First she'd lost Mother, and now Dad was dead. Didn't God see her pain? Didn't He care at all? Must the misery in her life keep on growing like yeast rising in bread?

She glanced around the kitchen, noting the faded yellow paint on the walls. The cream-colored linoleum was coming up in several places, and all the appliances were outdated. *Was I wrong to buy this place? If Dad were still alive, would he lecture me for spending my inheritance foolishly?*

The sound of a car door slamming shut drew Sinda's contemplations to a halt. It was probably Mrs. Kramer, since she only lived a mile away. *I'll worry about my ill-chosen spending some other time. Right now, I've got business to tend to.*

28

Glen stepped inside the back door, his arms full of groceries. He'd no more than set the bags on the table when Tara burst into the room. "Am I ever glad to see you!"

"Why, thank you, Miss Olsen. I'm happy to see you too." Glen rubbed his hands briskly together. "It's been a long Saturday, and after work I had to run some errands and grocery shop. Scoot on into the living room and tell Mrs. Mayer I'm home now. I'll put away the groceries, then we'll see what we can pull together for supper. What appeals to you, Honey? Tacos? Pizza?"

Tara tugged on his shirtsleeve. "I need to talk to you."

"In a minute," he said as he opened the first sack and withdrew a bag of apples. "Now do as I said."

Tara turned on her heels and was about to exit the room when Mrs. Mayer poked her head through the doorway. A radiant smile filled her broad face, and her pale blue eyes twinkled. Glen often thanked God for providing this pleasant, Christian woman to watch Tara every afternoon and on the Saturdays he was scheduled to work. "Do you need me to do anything else before I head for home?" the older woman asked.

Glen shook his head and placed the apples into the fruit bowl. "Can't think of a thing, Mrs. Mayer, thanks. Tara and I will see you at church tomorrow morning."

"Sure enough. Enjoy the rest of your evening." Mrs. Mayer waved her hand and exited through the back door.

Tara inched closer to her father. "Now can we talk?"

Glen put the perishable items in the refrigerator, then withdrew a carton of milk. "Are there any donuts left from the picnic you'd planned this afternoon with Penny, or did the two of you eat them all?" he asked, ignoring his daughter's perturbed look.

Tara shook her head. "We left a few, but Dad, we need to talk!"

Glen knew that Tara tended to be overly dramatic about most things. For some time now he had been trying to teach her to be patient and give him a chance to settle in so they could chat over a snack. Whatever she had to say could wait at least that long. "You get the donuts, and I'll pour us each a glass of milk. We'll sit at the table, and you can tell me what's on your mind. Then I've got to finish putting away the groceries and get busy making supper."

He started toward the table, but Tara halted his steps by positioning herself directly in front of him. "I think you should call the police."

Glen's eyebrows furrowed. "The police? What are you talking about?"

"Our neighbor. I'm talking about our new neighbor."

"Sinda?"

Tara's nose twitched as she pursed her lips. "She's the only new neighbor we have, isn't she?"

Glen frowned. "What's Sinda got to do with the police? Did she ask you to have me call them? Is she having some kind of problem?" Even though he didn't know Sinda very well, his heart squeezed at the thought of her being in some kind of trouble. "I'd better go over there and check on her."

He placed the carton of milk on the table and started for the back door.

"No, don't!" Tara's tone was pleading, and she grabbed his hand. "Let the police handle this, Dad."

"Handle what?"

Tara pointed at the table. "Sit down, and I'll tell you all about it."

As soon as they were both seated, Tara leaned forward with her elbows on the table, and in her most serious voice she announced, "There's a little kid in Sinda's house."

Glen drew in a deep breath and mentally counted to ten. "So there's a kid visiting Sinda. I see. And we should call the police because. . . ?"

"Sinda is buying and selling children!" Tara exclaimed. "That's against the law, and she's gotta be stopped."

Glen massaged the bridge of his nose. "Could we talk about this after dinner?"

"I'm telling you the truth!" Tara shouted. "Now, are you going to call the police or not?"

"What should I tell them?"

"Sinda is committing a crime. When people commit crimes, you're supposed to call the police."

He looked at her pointedly. "What crime has Sinda supposedly committed?"

"I just told you. She's buying and selling kids! I know of at least one who's locked in her basement right now."

Glen was tempted to laugh at the absurd accusation. "What were you watching on TV today?"

Tara gave him an icy stare. "I know what you're thinking, but I'm not making this up. That woman is a criminal."

"What sort of proof do you have?"

"I saw a lady bring a kid over to Sinda's house a little while ago. When the woman left, the kid wasn't with her."

Glen slowly shook his head. This story was getting better and better. "So tell me again, what is it that's illegal about baby-sitting someone's child?"

"Sinda drove off in her minivan a few minutes after the lady left, but the kid wasn't with her. She left it all alone in that creepy old house."

"Maybe you just didn't see the child leave with her."

"There's more, Dad."

"More?"

"I've been watching Sinda for several weeks now, and—"

"You mean spying, don't you?" Before Tara could respond, Glen rushed on. "I've warned you repeatedly about that—"

"But I've gathered some incriminating evidence," Tara interrupted.

Glen clicked his tongue. "Incriminating—such a big word for a little girl."

"Would you quit teasing and listen to me?" Tara demanded.

"Okay, okay," he conceded. "What incriminating evidence do you have on our new neighbor?"

"I've seen her bring other kids into that house." Tara frowned deeply. "Once she even brought in a baby who was in a wicker basket. I heard it crying." She paused a moment and swallowed hard. "Remember when Sinda first moved in and we went over to meet her and took her a plate of cookies?"

Glen nodded. "I remember."

"She was holding a doll when she opened the door, and she put it down really quick after she saw us. I thought maybe she had kids of her own, but then she told us she wasn't even married."

"So you naturally concluded that Sinda is up to no good." Glen shook his head. "What else haven't you told me?"

"I think that doll belonged to one of the kids she bought and sold. Today Penny and I saw Sinda and some lady with curly blond hair at the park. Sinda was telling the woman about her business, and she said she thought she was going to do okay because there are lots of kids in the world."

"Come on, Kiddo. You don't seriously think—"

"That's not all," Tara asserted. "Sinda keeps the children in her basement. I was checking her place out earlier, and I heard her talking on the phone. She was telling one of her customers that's where she puts them." Tara sucked in her breath. "Who knows how many innocent children are being held in that house, only to be sold on the black market?"

Glen leaned his head back and laughed. "Black market? You don't really expect me to believe that a nice woman like Sinda Shull is involved in something like that!"

"Yes, I do." Tara's eyes filled with tears.

Glen sat there for several seconds, trying to decide how best to handle the situation. His daughter had always been prone to exaggerate, but this story was a bit too much. Perhaps Tara's increasingly wild stories were just her way of getting his attention.

"Well, young lady," he finally said, "there seems to be only one way to settle the matter."

Her eyes brightened. "You're gonna call the cops?"

He shook his head. "No, I'm not. We are heading over to Sinda's. We're going to get to the bottom of this once and for all!"

six

A knock at the front door, followed by the sound of Sparky's frantic barking, drew Sinda out of the kitchen. She bent down and scooped the little dog into her arms and opened the door. She was surprised to discover Glen and Tara standing on her front porch. "What can I do for you?" she asked hesitantly.

Glen cleared his throat a couple of times and shuffled his feet. "There's a little matter I'd like to get cleared up. I'm sure it's just a silly misunderstanding, though."

"A misunderstanding?" Sinda repeated.

He nodded. "Tara—uh—thinks she's seen something going on over here."

Sinda alternated her weight from one foot to the other as she studied the fading rays of the evening sun dancing across Glen's jet-black hair. Her gaze roamed over his face next. He looked so nervous she almost felt sorry for him. "What do you think is going on?" she asked, shifting her gaze from Glen to his daughter.

"I want to know why you're buying and selling kids!" the child blurted out.

Sinda's mouth dropped open, and she blinked several times. "What?"

Tara narrowed her eyes in an icy stare. It was obvious by the tilt of her head and her crossed arms that the girl was not going to leave without some answers. "Don't try to deny it," Tara huffed. "I've been watching you. I know exactly what you're up to, and we're gonna call the police."

Glen backed away slightly, jamming his hands into the pockets of his blue jeans and staring down at the porch. "My detective daughter thinks you're involved with the black market."

Sinda could see that Glen was embarrassed, yet if there was

even a chance that he thought. . . She forced her attention back to Tara. "I imagine you've seen a few people come and go from my house with small children."

Tara's eyes widened and she nodded. "That's right, and you can't get away with a thing like that! See, Dad? She admits it!"

"You're an excellent detective," Sinda admitted.

Tara looked up at her father with a satisfied smile. "I told you. Now can we call the police?"

Glen groaned and slapped his palm against his forehead.

Sinda gently touched Tara's arm, but the child pulled away as though she'd been slapped. "I think you both should come inside and follow me."

"Follow you where?" Glen asked, lifting his dark eyebrows.

The intensity of his gaze sent shivers of apprehension up Sinda's spine. Was he angry? Should she be inviting them inside? Her mouth compressed into a tight line as she considered her options. Did she really want the police coming to her house? Police officers had made her feel uncomfortable ever since. . .

"Where do you want us to follow you to?"

Glen's deep voice invaded Sinda's thoughts, and she jerked her attention back to the situation at hand. "To my basement." She stepped onto the porch and set Sparky down. "Did you close the gate between our yards when you came over?"

Glen nodded, and Sinda motioned them inside. She led the way downstairs, and when they reached the bottom step she snapped on the overhead light.

Tara gasped and grabbed her dad's hand as the beam of light brought into view several small babies and two toddlers lying on a table in the center of the room.

"What in the world?" Glen's open mouth told Sinda how surprised he was by the unusual sight.

"I know this might appear a bit strange, but it's really quite simple." Sinda gestured toward the array of bodies. "You see, I'm a doll doctor, and these are my patients."

Tara's face turned ashen. "But, I–I thought—"

"The children you thought were coming and going from my house were dolls, Tara," Sinda explained. "I don't have my business sign nailed up on the house yet, but I do have a business license and a permit from the city to operate a doll hospital here."

Tara hung her head. "I–I guess I sort of got things mixed up."

"I would say so." Glen gave his daughter a nudge. "Don't you think you owe Sinda an apology?"

"It's all right. There was no harm done," Sinda said quickly. Despite Tara's accusation, she couldn't help but feel sorry for the child. Sinda had made her share of blunders when she was growing up, and Dad had never treated it lightly.

"Tara," Glen stated with a scowl on his face, "you owe Sinda an apology. We'll discuss the consequences of your behavior at home."

Tara continued to stare at the concrete floor. "I'm sorry, Sinda."

Sinda took a few steps toward the child. She wanted to give Tara a hug but didn't think it would be appreciated. Instead, she merely patted the child on top of her head. "It was an honest mistake. Any intelligent little girl could have gotten the wrong impression by what you saw."

Tara's head shot up. "I am not a little girl!"

"Good, then you won't mind doing some honest work to make up for your error," Glen asserted.

Tara's gaze darted to her dad. "What kind of work?"

Glen motioned toward Sinda. "I'm sure the doll doctor can find something for you to do right here in her workshop."

Sinda sucked in her lower lip. "I might be able to use some help." Although she wasn't sure she wanted the help to come in the form of a child's punishment.

"Dad, you know I don't play with dolls anymore," Tara said with a moan.

"You wouldn't be playing, Tara," Sinda insisted. "You'd be helping me with some necessary repairs."

Tara's eyes filled with sudden tears. "It's not fair. This old house is creepy, and I hate dolls!"

Glen bent down, so he was making direct eye contact with his daughter. "This case is closed, Tara."

❧

Glen stood in front of the dresser in his bedroom, studying Tara's most recent school picture. *She's such a cute kid, even though she can be a little stinker at times.* He drew in a deep breath as he reflected on the happenings of the evening. He should never have listened to Tara's crazy idea about Sinda selling kids on the black market, much less gone over there and made a complete fool of himself. He and Tara had been on their own for nine years, and it was hard not to indulge her. He knew he'd let her get too carried away, and tonight's fiasco made him realize how necessary it was to gain control. After they'd come home from Sinda's, he'd fixed dinner, seen to it that Tara did her weekend homework, then sent her to bed without any dessert. All her pouting, pleading, and crying over the idea of going to Sinda's to help repair dolls had nearly been his undoing, but Glen remained strong, even though he felt like an ogre.

As he moved toward the window and stared at the house next door, Glen's thoughts shifted to Sinda. He hadn't dated much since his wife's death, but of the few women he had gone out with, none had captured his interest the way Sinda had in the short time since they'd met. Some unseen pull made him want to seek out ways to spend more time with her. He wasn't sure if it was the need he sensed in her or merely physical attraction. The vulnerable side of Sinda drew him, but he would need to be cautious. She was like a jigsaw puzzle. So many pieces looked the same, but each time he tried to make them match, the pieces didn't fit. Sinda could be friendly one minute and downright rude the next. He had a hunch she was hiding something, only it was far beyond anything Tara had conjured up in her imagination. Glen's sixth sense told him that Sinda Shull had been hurt and might even be running from someone or something.

The fact that Sinda was a doll doctor had been a real surprise, but even more astonishing was that she'd given no evidence of her unusual occupation until Tara made her ridiculous accusations. Except for having dinner with them that one Sunday afternoon, Sinda had kept pretty much to herself.

"Sure wish I could get to know her better," Glen mumbled as he leaned against the windowpane. *Is Sinda a Christian?* He hoped so, because it would be wrong to begin a relationship with her if she wasn't. He raked a hand through his hair as confusion clouded his thinking. "I'd better pray about this before I approach Sinda with any questions about her faith."

∂

Sinda sat at the long metal table in her basement workshop, watching Tara sand an old doll leg. She couldn't help but notice the forlorn expression on the child's face, and without warning, vague memories from the past bobbed to the surface of her mind. She'd been sad most of her childhood. . .at least after her mother had gone. She'd tried hard to be the best daughter she could, but she'd apparently fallen short since she was never able to please her father.

I won't think about that now, she scolded herself. *I have work to do.* Quickly reaching for the doll head that went with the leg Tara was sanding, Sinda asked, "Do you recognize this doll?"

The girl's only response was a shake of her head.

"It's one of the original Shirley Temple dolls. It's a true collectable and quite valuable."

Tara squinted her dark eyes at Sinda. "You mean it's like an antique or something?"

Sinda nodded. "Right. See the cracks in her composition body?"

A glimmer of interest flashed across the young girl's face. "What's composition?"

"It's compressed sawdust and wood filler that's been poured into a mold. It has the look and feel of wood, but each part is actually hollow," Sinda explained. She ran her fingers gently along the antique doll's face, relishing in the notion that she had the power to transform an old relic into a work of art. "When composition ages, it often cracks or peels. Then it needs to be sanded, patched, and repainted."

"Who's Shirley Temple?" Tara asked as she continued to sand the doll leg.

"She was a child star who used to act in a lot of movies. When she became famous, the Ideal Toy Company created a line of dolls to look like her. Today, Shirley Temple dolls are worth a lot of money."

Tara shrugged, as though she'd become bored with the topic. "Say, where are you from, anyway?" she asked suddenly.

"I grew up in Seattle, Washington."

"Did you run a doll hospital there?"

Sinda nodded, then picked up a new wig for the doll and applied a thin layer of white glue to the bald head. "I took a home study course and started working on dolls when I was a teenager."

"Did you make lots of money? Enough to buy this creepy old house?"

Sinda clenched her teeth so hard her jaw ached. Tara's inquisition was beginning to get on her nerves. "I've never made enough money repairing dolls to entirely support myself, but after my dad died, I started buying and selling old dolls and a few other antiques."

"So, that's how you could afford this place?"

"My father left me his entire estate, and I used the money from the sale of our house in Seattle to purchase my new home and a minivan."

Tara's freckled nose crinkled, and Sinda was pretty sure more questions were forthcoming. "How come your dad didn't leave everything to your mother? Isn't that how it's supposed to be when a husband dies?"

Sinda's mouth fell open. She hadn't expected such a direct question, not even from her nosey little neighbor. "Uh—well— my mother's gone too." She secured the doll wig in place, fastened a rubber band around the head to keep it from slipping while it dried, then grabbed the other composition leg and gave it a few swipes with a piece of sandpaper.

"When did your mother die?" Tara prompted.

"She's been gone since I was ten."

"I was only a year old when my mother died, so I don't even remember her." Tara shrugged her slim shoulders. "If you have to lose someone, I guess that's the best way—when you're too young to remember."

Sinda's eyes filled with unexpected tears, and unable to stop the thoughts, her mind drifted back in time. Painful memories. So many painful memories. . .

Sinda had been small at the time. . .maybe five or six years old, but she remembered hearing a resonating cry waft through the house, followed by muffled sobs. She closed her eyes and saw herself halt on the stairs. There it was again. Her skin tingled, and her heart began to beat rapidly. A man and a woman were arguing. She held her breath. The woman's pleading escalated, then it abruptly stopped.

Silence.

Sinda's muscles tensed.

The woman screamed.

"What's wrong with Mama?" young Sinda had murmured. "Did she fall?" She hurried up the stairs. . .

Sinda felt a tug on the sleeve of her sweatshirt. She blinked several times, and the vision drifted slowly away. "What's wrong? I asked you a question, and you spaced off on me," Tara said, giving Sinda a curious stare.

"I–I must have been in deep thought."

"Yeah, I'll say."

"What was your question?"

"I was asking if your doll hospital did so well in Seattle, how come you moved to Oregon?"

Sinda frowned deeply. How many more questions was Tara going to fire at her? "I thought Elmwood would be a good place to start over," she answered through tight lips.

Tara leaned forward with her elbows on the table. "Why would you need to start over?"

Before Sinda could think of a reply, the telephone rang upstairs. She jumped to her feet, a sense of relief washing over her. "Keep working on that doll. I'll be right back," Sinda said, then she scurried up the steps.

seven

Several minutes later, Sinda hung up the phone. She smiled to herself. There was no telling when she might get another offer as good as the one she'd just had. The owner of a local antique shop wanted her to restore five old dolls. Two of them were bisque, and the other three were made of composition. The work was extensive and would bring in a fairly large sum of money. It looked as though Sinda's Doll Hospital was finally on its way.

Too bad Tara hates being here, she thought ruefully. *With all this extra work, I could probably use her help even after she's worked off her debt for spying on me. I wonder if she might be willing to extend the time if I offer some payment.*

Sinda crossed to the other side of the kitchen and opened a cupboard door. Tara might enjoy a treat, and it would certainly keep her too busy to ask any more personal questions.

She piled a few peanut butter cookies onto a plate, then filled a glass with cold milk. She placed the snack on a tray, picked up the cordless phone she'd left in the kitchen, and headed downstairs. She'd only descended two steps when she ran into Tara, nearly knocking the tray out of her hand.

"I–I heard a noise," the child squeaked.

Sinda's eyebrows furrowed. "What kind of noise?"

"A rustling sound. It was coming from one of the boxes over there." Tara pointed toward the wall lined with long shelves, but she never moved from her spot on the stairs.

"It's probably a mouse," Sinda said with a small laugh. "Should we go investigate?"

Tara's eyes grew wide. "No way!"

Sinda tipped her head to one side and listened. "Sparky's barking. Someone may be at the front door." She handed the tray to Tara. "Why don't you go back to the worktable and eat this snack? I'll be right down, then we'll check on that noise." She disappeared before Tara could argue the point.

When Sinda opened the front door, she discovered Glen standing on the porch. He held a loaf of gingerbread covered in plastic wrap. "This is for you," he said as Sparky darted between his legs and ran into the yard.

Little crinkles formed at the corners of his eyes when he smiled, and Sinda swallowed hard while she brushed a layer of sandpaper dust from the front of her overalls. *I wish he wouldn't look at me like that.* "Thanks, I love gingerbread," she murmured, taking the offered gift.

"Has anyone ever told you what gorgeous eyes you have?"

"What?" Sinda's heartbeat quickened.

"You have beautiful eyes."

She felt herself blush and knew it wasn't a delicate flush, but a searing red, covering her entire face. She quickly averted his gaze. "Shall I call Tara?"

Glen shook his head. "I didn't come over to get Tara."

"You—you didn't?" She glanced back up at him, feeling small and shy, like when she was a child. She wished he would quit staring at her. It filled her with a strange mixture of longing and fear.

"I came to bring you the bread, but I also wanted to ask you something."

"What did you want to ask?"

"Do you like Chinese?"

She stood there looking at him for several seconds, then realized he was waiting for her answer. "As in Chinese food?"

He nodded.

"I love Oriental cuisine."

He shuffled his feet a few times, bringing him a few inches closer. "I was wondering if you'd like to go out to dinner with me this Friday night."

Sinda could see the longing in Glen's eyes, and it frightened her. The scent of his aftershave stirred something deep inside her as well. "Just the two of us?" she rasped.

"Yep. I have other plans for my detective daughter."

Warning bells went off in Sinda's head. *Say no. Don't go out with Glen. Do not encourage him in any way!* When she opened her mouth to respond, the words that came out were quite different from those in her head, however. "I'd love to go."

Glen smacked his hands together, and she jumped. "Great! I'll pick you up around six-thirty." He bounded off the porch, calling, "Send Tara home when she's done for the day."

Sinda stood in the doorway, basking in the tingly sensation that danced through her veins. A question popped into her mind. *Would Dad approve of me going out with Glen Olsen?* She shook her head. *I shouldn't be thinking about Dad again.* Sinda was so innocent when it came to dealing with men, but she wanted to find out what Glen was really like. He appeared to be nice enough, but appearances could be deceiving. To the world her father had been a wonderful man, faithful in attending church, and attentive to Sinda's needs. But if Dad had truly loved God, wouldn't his actions at home have revealed it? Wasn't Christianity meant to be practiced in one's personal life, not just at church? As a child Sinda had practically worshiped her dad, but about the time she started into puberty she'd begun to question his motives. Driving the disturbing thoughts to the back of her mind, Sinda focused on the gingerbread Glen had given her. It needed to be put away.

When she returned to the basement, Sinda found Tara sitting on the third step from the bottom. She'd eaten all the cookies and was just finishing her milk. "What are you doing on the steps? I thought you would take the tray over to the table."

"I wasn't going near that box with the weird noise," Tara said, lifting her chin in defiance.

Sinda stepped around the child. "Let's go check it out."

Tara remained seated, arms folded across her chest as though daring Sinda to make her move. "You check it out. I'll wait here."

Sinda shrugged and started across the room. "And I thought you were a detective."

"I am!"

"Then come help."

Sinda glanced over her shoulder and was pleased to see Tara following her. However, it was obvious by the child's hunched shoulders and the scowl on her face that she was anything but thrilled about the prospect of trying to determine the nature of the strange noise.

When they came to the box in question, Tara stepped back as Sinda searched through the contents. "If it is a mouse, aren't you afraid it'll jump out and bite you?"

Sinda glanced over at Tara, who was cowering near the table. "I don't like mice, but I'm not afraid of them. I can't have a bunch of rodents chewing up my valuable doll parts."

"Why not set some traps?" Tara suggested. "That's what we used to do before we got Jake."

"Jake's your cat, right?"

"Yep, and he can get really feisty when there's a mouse around. I'd offer to lend him to you, but he wouldn't get along with your dog."

"You're probably right," Sinda agreed. She rummaged quickly through the rest of the doll parts, then set the box back on the shelf. "There's no sign of any mice. If there was one, it's gone now." She turned to face Tara. "That phone call I had earlier was an antique dealer. She has several old dolls for me to restore."

"Business is picking up, huh?"

Sinda nodded. "It would seem so, and I was wondering if you'd be interested in helping me here two or three afternoons a week."

"I thought I was helping."

"You are. I had a more permanent arrangement in mind," Sinda said. "Of course, I would pay you."

Tara frowned. "I don't like working with dolls. I'd much rather be watching TV or doin' some detective work."

"I really could use your help."

The child shook her head. "Not interested."

It was obvious that little Miss Olsen was not going to budge.

❧

"You're taking Sinda Shull where?" Tara shouted from across the room.

Glen was standing at the stove, stirring a pot of savory stew, but he turned to face his daughter. "I'm taking Sinda out to dinner, and I've arranged for you to stay overnight at Penny's."

Tara scowled at him. "This was Sinda's idea, wasn't it?"

"No, it was not her idea. I asked Sinda out when I took a loaf of gingerbread over there earlier today."

"What time was that?"

"Around four-thirty."

Tara tapped her toe against the linoleum. "I was over there then, and she never told me you stopped by. She didn't say she was going on a date with you either."

Glen turned back to the stove and started humming his favorite hymn, "Amazing Grace."

"Dad, why are you doing this?"

He kept on humming and stirring the stew.

Tara marched across the room and stopped next to the stove. "Why are you doing this?"

He winked at her. "Doing what?"

She grabbed his hand and gave it a shake. "Dad!"

He pushed her hand away. "Watch out, Tara. You're gonna fool around and get burned."

Tara took a step back, and she stared up at him accusingly. "Why did you invite Sinda to dinner?"

He smiled. "Because, it was the neighborly—"

"Thing to do," she said, finishing his sentence. "It's those green eyes of hers, isn't it?"

"What are you talking about?"

"I'll bet she's got you hypnotized. I saw it happen on a TV show once." Waving her hand in a crisscross motion, Tara said, "She zapped you senseless and put you under some kind of a spell."

Glen looked upward. "Oh, Lord, please give me the wisdom of Solomon." He wondered if he should lecture Tara about watching too much TV again, or would it be better to give her a Bible verse to memorize? After a few seconds' deliberation, he chose a different approach. "You're absolutely right, Kiddo. Sinda hypnotized me this afternoon. In fact, she put me so far under that I actually thought I was a dog."

"Dad, be serious! Sinda may not be buying and selling kids, but I don't trust her. I still think she's up to something."

"I would advise you to avoid detective work, Miss Olsen," he threatened. "Your last mistake got you thirty days of no TV and apprentice work in Sinda's Doll Hospital, remember?"

Tara's forehead wrinkled. "I'm too old to play with dolls, and Sinda's house is creepy and full of weird noises." She stomped her foot. "There's no way I'd keep working for her after my thirty days are up."

"She asked you to? What'd you tell her?" Glen asked with interest. If Tara kept working for their new neighbor, he might get to see Sinda more often. Besides, it would be a good way for Tara to learn about responsibility.

"I said no." Tara shrugged. "She offered to pay me, but I'm not going to spend my free time sanding and painting a bunch of old dolls!" She scrunched up her nose. "I'm going to discover Sinda's secrets, then we'll see who has the last laugh."

Glen chuckled. "We sure will, and it will probably be me."

eight

"Tara, it's time to go!" Glen called from the hallway outside his daughter's open bedroom door.

Tara slammed her suitcase lid shut when Glen stepped into the room.

"Would you like me to walk you over to Penny's?"

Tara shook her head. "I'm not a baby, Dad. You can just watch me walk across the street to Penny's if it makes you feel better."

Glen ran his fingers through his freshly combed hair. He thought the offer to walk with her might ease some of the tension between them. Ever since he'd told Tara about his date with Sinda, she'd been irritable. He straightened his tie and smoothed the lapel on his gray sport coat. "Do I look okay? I'm not overdressed, am I?"

"I guess it all depends on where you're goin'," Tara answered curtly. She sauntered out of the room, leaving her suitcase sitting on the floor.

Glen frowned but picked up the suitcase and followed. "I made reservations at the Silver Moon," he called after her.

Tara made no comment until she reached the bottom step. Then she turned and glared up at him. "I don't think you should go to the Silver Moon."

"Why not?"

"That place is too expensive!"

He smiled in response. "I'm sure I can scrape together enough money to pay for two dinners."

"How do you even know Sinda likes Chinese food?"

"She said so. What's this sudden concern about restaurant prices?" Glen exhaled a puff of frustration. He was not in the mood for this conversation.

She shrugged.

Glen bent down and planted a kiss on her forehead. "I'll watch you cross the street." He paused a moment. "Oh, and Tara?"

"Yeah, Dad?"

"You'd better behave yourself tonight."

She pursed her lips. "Don't I always?"

Glen knew it was time to get tough. He couldn't let Tara continue behaving like a spoiled, sassy brat. No matter how much he loved her or how sorry he was that she'd grown up without her mother, he had to remain firm. "I'm serious. You're already on restrictions, and if you pull anything funny at Penny's, I'll add another thirty days to your punishment."

Tara picked up her suitcase and marched out the front door. "Be careful tonight," she called. "Whatever you do, don't look directly into Sinda's weird green eyes!"

❧

Sinda paced between the fireplace and the grandfather clock. Glen wasn't late yet, but she almost hoped he would be. It would give her a few more minutes to compose herself. It had been almost three years since her last date, and that one had ended badly. She could still see the look on Todd Abernathy's face when her father gave him the third degree before they left for the theater. Even worse was when Todd brought her home and was about to kiss her good night. They'd been standing on the front porch, but the light wasn't on, so Sinda figured her father had gone to bed. She found out otherwise when he snapped on the porch light, jerked open the front door, and hollered, "You're late! I can't trust you on anything, can I?" His face was a mask of anger. "You're just like your mother, you know that?" It was the last time Todd ever came around.

Swallowing the pain, Sinda drove the unpleasant memories to the back of her mind and peered into the hallway mirror. Dad wouldn't be waiting for her tonight. If she embarrassed herself in front of Glen Olsen, it would be her own doing.

"I hope I look all right," she murmured as she studied her reflection. She'd chosen a rust-colored, full-length dress to wear and left her hair hanging long, pulled away from her face with a large beaded barrette at the nape of her neck. She didn't know what had possessed her to agree to this date, but she had, so there was no backing out now. When a knock at the front door sounded, her heart fluttered like a frightened baby bird. She drew in a deep breath as she moved to the hallway and reached for the doorknob.

Glen stood on the porch, dressed in a pair of black slacks, a white shirt with black pinstripes, and a gray jacket. He was smiling from ear to ear and holding a bouquet of pink and white carnations.

Sinda tried to smile but failed. Except for the corsage Dad had given her when she graduated from high school, no one had ever given her flowers before.

A crease formed between his brows. "You're not allergic to flowers, I hope."

"No, no, they're lovely. Let me put them in some water, then I'll be ready to go." Her voice was strained as his gaze probed hers. How could this man's presence affect her so?

Sinda left Glen waiting in the living room while she went to the kitchen to get a vase. When she returned a few minutes later, she found him with his hands stuffed inside his jacket pockets, strolling around the room. He seemed to be studying every nook and cranny. Sinda knew the wallpaper was peeling badly, the dark painted woodwork was chipped in several places, and the plastered ceiling needed to be patched and repainted. And this was just one room! The rest of the house was equally in need of repairs.

"The place is a mess," she said, placing the bouquet on a small antique table near her colonial-style couch.

Glen nodded and blew out his breath. "I'll bet nothing has been done to this old house in years."

Sinda shrugged. She didn't want to spoil the evening by talking about her albatross. "I'm ready to go if you are."

❧

The Silver Moon restaurant was bustling with activity, but

since Glen had made reservations, they were immediately ushered to a table. Like a true gentleman, Glen pulled out a chair for Sinda, then took the seat directly across from her.

She shifted uneasily, unsure of what to say, but was relieved when their waiter came and handed them each a menu. At least it gave her something to do with her hands.

"I'll think we'll have a plate of barbecued pork as an appetizer," Glen told the young man. He gestured toward Sinda. "Does that appeal to you?"

She licked her lips and struggled with words that wouldn't be a lie. At the moment, nothing appealed. *I probably shouldn't have accepted Glen's dinner invitation,* she silently berated herself. She was attracted to the man, and that worried her a lot. "Barbecued pork will be fine," she said with a nod.

When the waiter left, Glen leaned forward and smiled. "You look beautiful tonight."

Heat crept up Sinda's neck and flooded her face. "Thanks. You look nice too."

"Tell me, Doctor Shull, how's that daughter of mine doing in your doll hospital? Is Tara any help at all, or does she get in the way?"

Sinda smiled, and the tension in her neck muscles eased as she began to relax. "I don't think she likes the work, but she has been a big help. I even offered to pay her if she'd keep working for me a few afternoons a week."

Glen's blue eyes sparkled in the candlelight. "Tara told me."

Sinda laughed dryly. "She hated the idea and turned me down flat."

The waiter returned with a plate of barbecued pork surrounded by sesame seeds and a small dish of hot mustard.

Glen placed their dinner order, and as soon as the waiter left, he prayed his thanks for the food. Reaching for his glass of water, he said, "I have a proposition for you, Sinda."

"Oh?" She placed one hand against her stomach, hoping to calm the butterflies that seemed determined to tap dance the night away, and forced her ragged breathing to return to normal.

"It's a business proposition," he said in a serious tone.

A business proposition. Now that might be something to consider. "What kind of business proposition?"

"It's about doll repairing."

"You want to become a doll doctor?"

Glen had just popped a piece of pork into his mouth. He swallowed, coughed, and grabbed for his water again. "Too much mustard," he sputtered.

Sinda bit back a smile. "That's why I prefer ketchup."

"I'm afraid I wouldn't make much of a doll doctor," Glen said after his fit of coughing subsided.

"Why not? I've read about some men who repair dolls in one of my doll magazines."

He nodded. "I'm sure that's true, but it isn't what I had in mind."

"What then?"

"Tara's mother had an old doll that belonged to her grandmother. The doll's been in a box under my bed for years. Tara doesn't even know about it."

"It could be quite valuable."

"I don't know about that, but it does need fixing. When Tara was born, Connie was so excited about having a little girl. She was sure she'd be able to pass the old doll down to our daughter someday." Glen's face was pinched with obvious pain. "Of course that never happened. Connie died a year later."

"It's not too late. You can still give Tara the doll her mother wanted her to have," Sinda said softly.

"I never gave it to her before because I didn't know where to take it for repairs."

"And now you do," she said with a smile. "So, what's the proposition you had in mind?"

Glen took a sip of his hot tea before answering. "The doll's a mess, and I'm sure it'll be expensive to fix." He massaged the bridge of his nose and grimaced. "I'm not even sure it's worth fixing—especially since my daughter isn't too thrilled about dolls these days."

"I'm certain that once Tara finds out it was her mother's, she'll be glad to have it."

"I was thinking maybe we could trade services in payment."

Her eyebrows shot up. "What service might you have to offer me?"

He grinned. "Your place could use a few repairs and some fresh paint. I'm pretty handy with a paintbrush. My carpentry skills aren't half bad either."

It only took Sinda a few seconds to think about his offer. Except for some new kitchen curtains Carol had helped her make, she hadn't done much in the way of fixing up the old place. "I do need some work done." She drew in a deep breath and expelled it quickly. "Without seeing the doll and assessing an estimate to restore it, I can't be sure our trade would be a fair one."

"I'm sure you can find enough work for me to do, should the cost be too high."

Sinda suppressed a giggle. "I didn't mean the price of the doll repairs would be too high. I meant the amount of work I need to have done far exceeds anything I could ever do for one antique doll."

Glen eyed her curiously. "I'm not concerned about balancing it out. If I come up short on the deal, maybe you can even things out a bit by agreeing to cook me dinner sometime."

Sinda reached for a piece of pork. What was there about Glen that made her feel so comfortable? Did she dare allow herself to begin a relationship with him—even a working one? She popped the meat into her mouth, wiped her fingers on her napkin, and extended her hand across the table. "You've got yourself a deal."

He looked pleased. At least she thought it was a look of pleasure she saw on his face. Maybe he had indigestion and was merely trying to be polite.

nine

"Thanks for the nice evening, Glen. I ate so much I probably won't need to eat again all weekend." Sinda leaned her head against the vinyl headrest in the front seat of Glen's station wagon and sighed deeply.

"It doesn't have to end yet," he said, a promising gleam in his eyes. "We could take a drive out to Elmwood Lake. It's beautiful there in the spring."

With only a slight hesitation, she gave her consent. *What am I doing?* an inner voice warned. *I should really go home.*

Glen turned on the radio and slipped a cassette into place. The rich, melodious strains of a Christian gospel singer poured from the speakers. "This song, about our soul finding rest, is one of my favorites," he commented.

Sinda closed her eyes and let the music wash over her like a gentle waterfall. It had been so long since she'd listened to any kind of Christian music, and the tape had such a calming effect. "Umm. . .I do enjoy this type of music."

By the time the song ended, Glen had pulled into the parking lot. "We still have a hint of daylight. Want to take a walk around the lake?"

"That sounds nice. I need to work off some of my dinner," Sinda said with a nervous laugh. *I really should be home in bed. . .or working on a doll. . .any place but here.*

"It's getting kind of chilly," Glen remarked. "Want to wear my jacket?"

She shook her head. "No thanks, I'm fine."

They walked along quietly for awhile, then Glen broke the silence. "I was wondering if you'd like to go to church on Sunday with me and Tara."

Sinda's shoulders sagged, and she shook her head. "Thanks

for asking, but I'd better not."

"Have you already found a church home?"

She stopped walking and turned to face him. "What makes you think I'm a churchgoer?"

He studied her intently for a few seconds. "I—uh—saw an old Bible on your coffee table, so I just assumed—"

"Looks can be deceiving."

He drew back, as though she'd offended him, and she started walking again, a little faster this time.

"You're upset about something, aren't you?" Glen asked when he caught up to her.

A curt nod was all she could manage.

"What is it? What's wrong?"

Unexpected tears spilled over, and she blinked several times trying to dispel them.

Suddenly, Sinda's steps were halted as Glen drew her into his arms. "Are you angry with me?"

"No," she muttered against his jacket. She couldn't tell him what was really bothering her.

He pulled slightly away and lifted her chin with his thumb. "It might help to talk about it."

She sniffed deeply and took a step back. "I'd rather not."

"Maybe some other time."

She shrugged. "Maybe."

Then, as if the topic of church had never been mentioned, Glen changed the subject. "So, when would you like to begin?"

She blinked. "Begin?"

"On your house repairs?"

"Oh. I guess you can start whenever it's convenient. When can I take a look at the doll?"

"Whenever it's convenient," he said with a deep chuckle. "How about tonight? Tara's staying over at her friend Penny's, so it would be the perfect time to show you."

Sinda shivered and rubbed her hands briskly over her bare arms. "I suppose that would be all right."

"You are cold." Glen draped one arm across her shoulders,

and she shivered again, only this time she knew it wasn't from the cold.

"Tara mentioned that you moved here from Seattle," Glen remarked. "She said you used to run a doll hospital there too."

Sinda nodded. *I wonder what else Tara told her dad.*

"I understand your father passed away, and your mother died when you were Tara's age?"

Sinda skidded to a stop. The camaraderie they'd begun to share had been blown away like a puff of smoke. "We've certainly done our homework, haven't we? I guess your daughter isn't the only detective in the family."

"She is the only one. At least, she thinks she is." Glen chuckled, apparently unaware of her annoyance.

"If you wanted a rundown on my past, why not ask me yourself?" she snapped. "Wouldn't it have been better than getting secondhand information from a child?"

"I did not ask my daughter to get the lowdown on you. She volunteered it—plain and simple."

Glen's tone had cooled some, and Sinda suddenly felt like an idiot. Maybe she was making a big deal out of his questions. Perhaps Dad had taught her too well about keeping to herself. "I guess I jumped to conclusions," Sinda said apologetically. "I think that's enough about me for one night, anyway. Why don't you tell me something about yourself?"

"Let's see now. . .I'm thirty-four years old. I've been a Christian since I was twelve. My parents are missionaries in New Guinea. I have one brother, who is two years younger than me. I'm a mailman who loves his job but hates the blisters he gets when he wears new boots. I love to look for bargains at yard sales and thrift stores. I've been a widower for nine years. My daughter is the official neighborhood snoop, and I'm the best cook in Elmwood, Oregon." He wiggled his eyebrows. "Anything else you'd like to know?"

Sinda couldn't help but smile. She and Glen Olsen had more in common than she would have guessed. At least she liked yard sales and thrift shops, and they did enjoy the same kind of music and eating Chinese food. Glen was like a breath of fresh air—able to make her smile and even temporarily forget the pain from her past. "How come a good-looking, great cook like you has never remarried?" she asked.

"I have dated a few women since my wife's death," he acknowledged. "I was in too much pain the first few years to even think about another woman, but when I did finally start dating, Tara didn't like it." He reached for Sinda's hand and gave it a gentle squeeze. "To be perfectly honest, until recently I've never met a woman besides my wife, Connie, who could hold my interest."

Until recently? Did he mean her? Dare she ask? She was about to, but he threw a question at her instead.

"How about you? Have there been many men in your life?"

She shook her head, hoping, almost praying, he wouldn't pursue the subject. "It's getting dark. Maybe we should go. You did say you wanted me to take a look at that doll, right?"

Glen nodded, and they turned back toward his car.

❧

Sinda waited in the living room while Glen went upstairs to get the doll. When he returned a short time later, she was standing in front of the fireplace, looking at a photograph on the mantel.

"That was the last picture ever taken of Connie," he said, stepping up beside Sinda. "It was about a year before she died."

She placed the photograph back on the mantel. "She was lovely."

A few tears shimmered in Glen's sapphire blue eyes as he replied, "Her sweet attitude and Christian faith never wavered—not even when the end came near."

Sinda swallowed hard, trying not to feel his pain, yet in spite of her resolve, her heart went out to Glen. What would it be like to raise a child alone? Her father knew, but she'd never asked him. She hadn't dared to ask any personal questions, especially about her mother.

Yanking her attention away from the captivating, dark-eyed

brunette in the picture, Sinda leaned over the coffee table to examine the old doll Glen had placed there.

The bisque-head, ball-jointed doll lay in pieces, and the blond mohair wig was nearly threadbare. Several fingers and toes were missing as well. Sinda held the head gently, turning it over to see if it had any special markings that might indicate who had made it. "Ah. . .a German doll," she murmured. "She's quite old and a real treasure."

"You mean the doll could be worth something?" he asked, lifting his eyebrows in obvious surprise.

"Several hundred dollars, I'd say."

Glen frowned. "It needs a lot of work, though."

She shrugged her shoulders. "Nothing I haven't done before."

"How long do you think it would take?"

"Probably a month or two."

He nodded and gave her another one of his heart-melting smiles. "Then for the next month you'll have my handyman services." They shook on it to make it official, and Sinda said she should be getting home.

As Glen walked her next door, Sinda could hear Sparky barking from inside the house.

"Be quiet, you dumb dog. You'll alert the whole neighborhood," a child's shrill voice hissed.

"Alert them to what?" Glen bellowed.

Tara, who was crouched in one corner of Sinda's front porch, jumped in obvious surprise, and so did Sinda. "Dad! What are you doing here?"

"I think the question should be 'What are you doing here, Miss Olsen?' Aren't you supposed to be at Penny's?"

Tara rocked back and forth on her heels, clasping her hands tightly together. "I–I—that is—"

Sinda's gaze swung from Tara, to Glen, to a strange-looking object on her front porch. She leaned over for a closer look. "Where did this old trunk come from?" she asked, glancing back at Tara.

The child rubbed the palms of her hands over her blue jeans and licked her lips before she replied. "I—uh—was upstairs in Penny's room, and I happened to glance out the window, when—"

"I'll bet you just happened to," Glen interrupted.

"Go on, Tara," Sinda prompted.

At her father's nod, Tara touched the trunk with the toe of her sneaker and continued. "I saw a dark-colored van pull into your driveway. A man got out, and he took this big thing out of the back. He carried it up the walk and set it on your front porch. Then he knocked on the door, but when nobody answered, he left it and drove away."

"Did you get a good look at the man? Did you see any markings on the van or anything that might give us some clue?" Glen questioned.

Tara shook her head. "No, but I decided to come over here and see if he left a note or anything."

Sinda dropped to her knees beside the trunk. She thought she recognized it, but under the dim porch light she couldn't be sure. "There's a shipping tag attached to the side. It has my name and address on it." She glanced up at Tara. "The man you saw was probably from the freight company who sent the trunk."

"Who's it from, and what's inside?" Tara asked excitedly.

"That is none of our business, young lady." Glen offered Sinda his hand, and she stood up again. "That thing looks kind of heavy. Want me to carry it into the house for you?"

"I'd appreciate it," she replied.

Glen pointed at Tara. "Get on back to Penny's. We're going to have a little talk about this in the morning."

Tara bounded off the porch, but she turned back when she reached the sidewalk. "Say, Dad, what's in that cardboard box you're holding?"

Glen nodded in the direction of Penny's house. "Go!"

Sinda waited until Tara was safely across the street and had entered her friend's house before she opened the front door.

Glen handed Sinda the box with the antique doll in it, then he hoisted the trunk to his broad shoulders and followed her inside.

At her suggestion, Glen set the trunk in the hallway, then moved toward the door, hesitating slightly. To her surprise, he lifted his hand and gently touched the side of her face, sending shivers of delight up her spine. She breathed in the musky scent of his aftershave and held her breath as he bent his head toward her. Their lips touched briefly in a warm kiss as delicate as butterfly wings.

"I guess I should apologize for that," Glen whispered when he pulled away. "I'm not usually so forward."

Sinda's cheeks flamed as she realized how much she'd enjoyed the brief kiss. "Good night, Glen," was all she managed to say.

With hands in his pocket and shoulders slightly slumped, Glen ambled out the front door. Did he think she was angry? Should she have said something more?

Sinda shut the door, shuffled to the living room, and slumped to the couch with a groan. She sat there, staring vacantly at the unlit fireplace, then reached up to touch her mouth, still feeling the warmth of Glen's lips. As extraordinary as the kiss felt, she could never let it happen again!

She closed her eyes momentarily, and when she opened them, her gaze rested on the massive trunk sitting in the hallway. Who sent it and why? Should she open it now or wait until morning?

Sinda forced herself to get up from the couch, and she moved slowly across the room. *Why put off until tomorrow what you can do today?* She could hear her father's words as if he were standing right beside her. How many times had he reprimanded her for procrastinating? How many times had he screamed at her for forgetting things? Why was it so important to do things right away? Worse yet, why was she still doing things his way? He was dead. Shouldn't she be able to make her own decisions and do things her way?

"I guess old habits die hard," Sinda said as she knelt beside the trunk. With trembling fingers she grasped the handle and pulled. It didn't budge. That's when she noticed the hasp was held securely in place by a padlock. The key! Where was the key?

It had been many years since Sinda had seen the trunk, though she'd never viewed any of its contents. She was certain it was her mother's trunk, which she'd seen in her closet on several occasions. She'd always figured Dad had thrown it out after Mother left. Seeing it now was a painful reminder that her mother was gone forever. It made her feel as if she were ten years old again. . .sad, betrayed, and confused by everything that had happened.

Driving the troubling thoughts to the back of her mind, Sinda directed her focus to the old trunk. On closer examination, she discovered a business card attached to the handle. A light finally dawned. Alex Masters, their family lawyer, must have had access to the trunk, for it was his name and address inscribed on the card.

Without a key Sinda had no way of getting into the trunk tonight. She may as well go up to bed. In the morning she'd give Alex a call and see if he had the key. She was in no hurry to open up old wounds, anyway. There were too many hurts from her past, and after such a lovely evening with Glen, she would rather not think about them.

ten

It was Saturday morning, and Tara, recently home from Penny's, had been sent outside to do more weeding in the flowerbeds. Glen watched her wipe the dampness from her forehead and heard her mutter, "If my mother was still alive, she'd be out here in the garden with me. Dad wouldn't be acting so goofy around our weird neighbor, either."

"Who are you talking to?" Glen tapped his daughter on the shoulder, and she whirled around to face him.

"Myself." She glanced at the toolbox in his hand. "What's that for?"

"Starting today I'll be helping Sinda do some repairs on her house during my free time, so if you need me just give a holler."

Tara's mouth dropped open like a broken hinge. "I thought you and I were goin' shopping today. Summer will be here soon, and I need new clothes."

Glen shrugged. "I had planned to take you to Fuller's Mall, but since you snuck out of Penny's house last night, you'll be spending the entire day doing chores. I've also decided that when your time is up at Sinda's, you can do another thirty days of doll repairs." Tara's eyes widened, and he drew in a deep breath, wondering if he was being too hard on her. He knew he was lenient at times, but there were other times, like right now, when he snapped like a turtle. *I have good reason to be stern with her,* he reasoned. *Tara disobeyed me, in spite of my warnings.*

Tara looked up at him as though she might burst into tears, and he chastised himself for feeling guilty. He leveled her with a look he hoped was admonishing. "If Sinda and I ever go out again, you'll be staying with Mrs. Mayer or at Uncle Phil's."

Tara thrust out her chin. "Aw, Dad, Uncle Phil lives in a dinky little apartment. He has no kids, and there's never anything fun to do there."

Glen couldn't argue with that. His younger, unmarried brother had his own successful business and was hardly ever home, so Phil didn't need a large place to live.

Tara's lower lip protruded. "And I don't see why I have to do more work for that weir—"

"Don't even say it," Glen interrupted. He motioned toward the flower beds. "When you're done weeding here, you can start out front."

"But, I did those a few weeks ago," she argued.

"Then do them again!" Glen disappeared, forcing all thoughts of his disobedient daughter to the back of his mind. Right now, all he wanted to do was get over to Sinda's and start working.

He opened the gate and trudged through her overgrown yard. *I should offer to mow this mess.* Glen set the toolbox on Sinda's porch and knocked on her back door. She opened it right away, but he was disappointed when she didn't return his smile. She was wearing a pair of dark green overalls and a pale green T-shirt that deepened the color of her eyes, and her hair was pulled up into a ponytail. A strange sensation spread through Glen's chest. Despite her casual attire and sullen expression, he thought she looked beautiful.

"Good morning, Glen," Sinda said with downcast eyes. What was wrong? Why wouldn't she look at him?

"Morning," he responded cheerfully. He hoped his positive mood might rub off on her. "You have my services for most of the day, so where would you like me to begin?"

"You sound rather anxious to work up a sweat on such a warm spring day."

"Just keeping true to my word." He gave her a quick wink, but there was no response. Not even a smile. *It might be that she's upset because Tara was snooping around on her front porch last night. Or maybe it was that unplanned kiss. Should I ask?*

"I haven't started on your wife's old doll yet," Sinda said, breaking into Glen's contemplations.

He shrugged. "I just gave it to you last night."

"Before you tackle any of my house repairs, would you mind moving that old trunk upstairs?" she asked, changing the subject.

"No problem." He stepped inside, hoisted the trunk to his shoulders, and followed Sinda up the stairs.

When they came to the first room, she moved aside. "This room is full of boxes and things I haven't had time to find a place for yet, so let's put it here." She frowned deeply. "I don't even have a key that will open the trunk."

Glen raised his eyebrows. "No key came with it?"

She shook her head. "I have several old keys with some of my antiques, but nothing fits. I found my lawyer's business card on the handle last night, so I'll contact him to see if he has the key."

"Would you like me to break it open? I don't think it would be too difficult."

At first Sinda looked as though she might be considering the offer, but to his surprise she replied, "I'll wait and see what my lawyer has to say. There's no sense ruining a perfectly good padlock if it's not necessary."

Glen turned toward the door. "Where would you like me to begin? Should I start by mowing the lawn?"

"I think I can handle that myself," she said. "Why don't you try to do something about the front porch? It's even more dilapidated than the back porch, and since my customers come to the front door, I'd rather not have someone trip on a loose board and sue me for everything I don't own."

The expression on her face softened, and it made Glen's heart race. He grinned and started back down the stairs with Sinda following on his heels. He was glad the tension he'd felt when he first arrived seemed to be abating. "By the time you finish your breakfast, I should have a fairly good start on the project."

Her forehead wrinkled. "How'd you know I was about to eat breakfast?"

They were at the bottom of the stairs now, and Glen turned to face her. "My daughter's always telling me that I'm the best cook in the world. What kind of cook would I be if I couldn't smell scrambled eggs and sausage?"

Sinda grimaced and covered her face with her hands. "Guess I'm caught. If you haven't eaten yet, you're welcome to join me."

Glen held his stomach and gave her what he hoped was his best grin. He'd eaten a bowl of cereal and a piece of toast around seven, and it was a little after nine now. He could probably eat again.

❧

"Please, Dad, not another Sunday dinner with Sinda!"

Glen was putting away the leftovers from their Saturday evening supper of pizza and salad, while Tara cleared the table.

"Tara Mae Olsen, what is wrong with you? It seems like all you do anymore is whine and complain. What is your problem?"

"It's actually your problem, Dad, not mine," she answered sullenly.

"What is that supposed to mean?"

"Sinda's the problem, not me." Now Tara looked like she was going to cry, and she flopped into a chair and lowered her head to the table.

Glen took the seat across from her and reached out to take her hand, suddenly feeling like a big heel. He hadn't meant to make her cry. "What kind of problem do you see attached to Sinda Shull?"

Tara's head shot up, and tears rolled down her cheeks. "Can't you see it, Dad. She's out to get you."

His mouth dropped open. "You actually think Sinda is out to get me?"

The pathetic look on Tara's face told him that was exactly what she thought.

"I saw her kiss you last night."

Glen's ears were burning. He didn't see how Tara could have known they were kissing. He'd seen her go into Penny's house. Furthermore, he and Sinda had kissed when they were standing in the hallway, in front of the door. Maybe she was only guessing. She was pretty good at that.

Tara stared at the table, her lower lip quivering like a leaf in the wind. "Just how did you manage to see us kissing?"

She sniffed deeply. "I was looking out Penny's bedroom window."

"It was dark when you went back to the Spauldings'," Glen reminded. "And Sinda and I were. . ." He paused and reached up to scratch the back of his head. "You were using those binoculars again, weren't you?"

Tara's face turned pink.

"How many times have I told you to stop spying on people?"

"I wasn't exactly spying," she defended. "I was looking outside. The binoculars just picked you up through that little window in Sinda's front door."

"First, you need to give those binoculars to me until you show yourself trustworthy and ready to respect others' privacy. Second, for the record, Sinda did not kiss me. It was the other way around."

Tara jumped out of her seat, nearly knocking the chair over. "Dad, how could you do such a thing? You hardly even know her!"

"I know her well enough to realize I enjoy her company." He shrugged. "Besides, it's no big deal. It was just an innocent good night kiss." *One that shouldn't have happened,* his conscience reminded. *Sinda refused your invitation to church, and you still don't know if she's ever had a personal relationship with Christ.*

"She's got you hypnotized!"

"Don't start that again, Tara. I'm in perfect control of my faculties." But even as he spoke the words Glen wondered if they were true. Not that he believed he'd actually been hypnotized by Sinda's green eyes. But there was something about the woman that held him captive. Whenever he was with Sinda he had a strange sense of some kind of mystery awaiting him. It was exciting and troubling at the same time.

"The Bible tells us to love our neighbors as ourselves, and I've invited Sinda to come for Sunday dinner again," he said with authority. "She's graciously accepted, and you will be gracious to our dinner guest. Is that clear?"

Tara hung her head. "Yeah, I understand. I wish you did."

❧

Sinda sat at her kitchen table, toying with the piece of salmon on her plate. She loved fish, especially salmon. Tonight she had no appetite, though. She hadn't been able to reach Alex Masters by phone today, and she had mixed feelings about it. Since this was Saturday, her lawyer obviously wasn't in his office, but she'd also gotten his answering machine at home. Even though she wasn't thrilled about the prospect of opening the trunk, there was a part of her that wanted to see what was inside. If it was her mother's trunk, maybe there was something within the contents that could help heal some of her pain.

Resigned to the fact that she'd have to wait until next week to call Alex again, Sinda let her thoughts carry her in another direction. Against her better judgment she had accepted another dinner invitation from Glen. She felt apprehensive about going—especially since she knew better than to allow herself to get close to a man.

Sinda thought about how Glen had spent most of the day working on her house. He'd replaced rotten boards on the front porch steps, repaired a broken railing, and helped her strip the torn wallpaper in the dining room. Then, shortly before he left, he had extended the dinner invitation. Sinda had been so appreciative of all this work that she'd accepted without even thinking.

What kind of power does that man hold over me? she fumed. *I should know better than to let my guard down because Glen seems kind and is easy to talk to. By his actions he appears to be nice, but is he all he claims to be?*

Sirens in the distance drove Sinda's thoughts unwillingly back to the past. Whenever she heard that shrill whine she remembered the frightening night when the police showed up at their door, demanding to know if someone had been injured. Sinda had heard one of the police officers say they'd had a report from a neighbor about hearing loud voices coming from the Shulls' home. Dad was able to convince the officer that everything was fine, and the shouting the neighbor heard was probably just the TV turned up too loud. Sinda remembered hearing her parents hollering at each other that night. Of course, that had been a regular occurrence, even though her mother always assured her there was nothing to worry about.

As the sound of the sirens diminished, so did Sinda's thoughts from the past. She jabbed at the fish on her plate and exclaimed, "I'll go to dinner tomorrow because I promised, but after that I won't accept any more social invitations from Glen!"

eleven

As Sinda rang the Olsens' doorbell the following day, she noticed that she felt a bit more relaxed than she had the previous time she'd come to dinner. Not only did she know Glen and Tara better, but she had a sense of peace about her decision last night. She would try to be a good neighbor, but nothing more.

When Tara opened the front door, the distinctive aroma of oregano assaulted Sinda's senses, and she sniffed the air. "Something smells good."

"Dad's fixing spaghetti."

"I love most any kind of pasta dish." Sinda stepped inside, even though she hadn't been invited.

Tara gave her an icy stare, but she led the way to the kitchen without another word. When Glen turned from the stove and offered her a warm smile, Sinda squeezed her lips together to keep her mouth from falling open. How could any man look so good or so masculine when he was wearing an oversized apron and holding a wooden spoon in one hand?

"You're right on time. Dinner's almost ready, and I thought we'd eat in here." Glen nodded toward the kitchen table, which had already been set.

"Is there anything I can do to help?" Sinda asked hopefully. Anything would be better than standing here like a ninny, gawking at Glen and wishing. . . What was she wishing for anyway?

Using his spoon, Glen motioned toward the table. "Have a seat, and we can talk while I finish dishing things up." He glanced at Tara, who was leaning against the cupboard with her arms folded across her chest. "Honey, would you please fill the glasses with water?"

The child did as he requested, but Sinda could tell by Tara's deep sigh and slow movements that she was not happy about it.

"Your kitchen looks so clean and orderly." Sinda laughed self-consciously. "I love to cook, but you should see my kitchen clutter after I'm done with a meal. It looks like a tornado blew in from the east."

Glen chuckled. "I wasn't always this efficient. I've had lots of practice, and lots of help from Tara, which is probably why I appear so capable."

Sinda toyed with the fork lying beside her plate. "I've been cooking since I was a young girl, and I still make messes. I guess some people tend to be neater than others."

Tara came to Sinda's water glass, and Sinda quickly moved to one side, barely in time to avoid being caught in the dribbles that weren't quite making it into her glass. "Sorry about that," the child mumbled.

"Tara, why don't you go out to the living room until dinner is served?"

"There's nothing to do out there," the child moaned. "I can't watch TV, and—"

"Read a book or play with Jake. Sinda and I want to visit."

Tara stomped out of the room, and Glen turned to face Sinda. "Returning to our discussion about your cooking abilities—I thought the breakfast you fixed yesterday tasted great, and I never even looked at your kitchen clutter."

Sinda grimaced. "That meal wasn't much to write home about."

"Maybe you'd like the chance to cook a real meal for me. Then I can judge for myself how well you cook." Glen winked at her. "And I promise not to critique your cleaning skills."

Sinda felt her face flame as she sat there silently watching his nimble fingers drop angel-hair pasta into the pot of boiling water on the stove. When he finished, he looked her way again. "Guess a guy shouldn't go around inviting himself to dinner, huh?"

"It's not that," Sinda was quick to say. "It's just—I've been thinking maybe we might be seeing too much of each other."

"I enjoy your company, and I kind of hoped you liked being with me. After all, we both like to cook, love to go to yard sales and thrift stores, and even enjoy the same kind of relaxing music." A deep, crescent-shaped dimple sprang out on the right side of Glen's mouth as he smiled. Funny, she'd never noticed it before.

Sinda's face grew even warmer. "I do enjoy being with you, Glen, but—"

"Then let's get better acquainted."

Sinda could feel her resolve fly right out the window, and she swallowed hard. Glen was right; they did have a few things in common. "Maybe we can try dinner at my house next Sunday. Tara's invited too, of course," she added quickly.

"Sounds great, and the invitation to attend church with us is still open if you're interested."

Sinda's heart began to race, and she wasn't sure if it was Glen's smile or the mention of church. "I think it would be best to stick with dinner," she said, feeling as though she couldn't quite get her breath.

"I was hoping you might have changed your mind about going to church."

Sinda reached for her glass and took a sip of water before she answered. "I went to church every Sunday with my dad."

"Did you ever commit your life to Christ?"

She nodded slowly. "When I was ten years old and went to Bible school, I accepted Jesus as my Savior." Was that a look of relief she saw on Glen's face?

"That's great, and it gives us one more thing in common." He frowned slightly. "So, if you're a Christian, how come you're not interested in finding a church home?"

Sinda licked her lips, searching for the right words. How could she tell Glen, a man she was just getting to know, what had happened to her faith in God? "I—uh—could we please change the subject?"

Glen nodded and began to drain the spaghetti into the

strainer he'd placed in the sink. "Is there anything you'd like me to bring to dinner next Sunday. . .maybe some dessert?"

You are dessert, Glen Olsen. It's just too bad I'm on a diet, Sinda thought as she shrugged her shoulders. "Some dessert would be nice."

≈

The following week, Sinda became even more fretful than usual. It wasn't until Thursday when she finally heard from her lawyer. Then it was only to say that he'd been on vacation when she'd called. When Sinda questioned him about the trunk, he informed her that it had been in storage for several years. Though not mentioned in the will, it was her father's verbal request that she should have it after he died. Alex had forgotten all about the trunk until a bill arrived from the storage company a few weeks ago. When she asked him about the key, he said he hadn't been given one.

Wondering if she should break the lock or keep looking for a key that might fit, Sinda decided to do nothing for the time being. She wasn't even sure she wanted to see the contents of the trunk, so maybe more time was what she needed.

Another reason for Sinda's stress was Tara Olsen. The child's most recent act of disobedience had extended her time working in Sinda's doll hospital to another four weeks. While Sinda did appreciate the extra help, having Tara around seemed to add to her problems. She had to be extra careful not to let the girl see the antique doll Glen had asked her to repair. She'd have to do those restorations whenever Tara wasn't around. The sullen child was also sneaking around, nosing into places that were none of her business. Sinda had no idea what the would-be detective was looking for, but it irritated her, nonetheless.

Today was Saturday, and Tara was in the basement, cleaning the body of an ink-stained vinyl doll. Glen was up on the second floor, working in the bathroom, and Sinda was in the kitchen, making a pitcher of iced tea. She could hear him moving around overhead—a thump here—the piercing whine of a drill there. She could only imagine how he must look right now, bent over the sink, tools in hand, trying to make it usable.

Sinda placed the tea in the refrigerator and opened the basement door. She had to check on Tara and quit thinking about Glen Olsen!

When she entered the doll hospital a few minutes later, Sinda found Tara scrubbing the stomach of the vinyl doll with diluted bleach and a toothbrush, an effective treatment for ink stains.

"How's it going?" Sinda asked, peering over the child's shoulder.

Tara shrugged. "Okay, I guess."

"Have you heard any more strange noises down here?"

"Not today, but I still think this old house is creepy. Aren't you afraid to live here alone?"

Sinda shook her head. Even if she were a bit apprehensive at times, she'd never admit it to Tara. She sat down in the chair on the other side of the table. "I have Sparky for protection, so there's no reason to be afraid."

Tara lifted her gaze to the ceiling. "You'd never catch me living in a place like this."

"Maybe when your dad's finished with the critical repairs it will look less creepy."

Tara's head lurched forward as she let out a reverberating sneeze.

Sinda felt immediate concern. "Is that bleach smell getting to you?"

Tara sneezed again. "I think it is."

"Why don't you set it aside and work on something else?" Sinda placed the doll on a shelf and handed Tara another one. "This little lady needs her hair washed and combed." She gave the child a bottle of dry shampoo, used expressly for wigs. "You can work on it while I run upstairs and tend to a few things. I'll call you in about fifteen minutes, then we can have a snack. How's that sound?"

"Whatever," Tara mumbled.

⋙

Glen leaned over the antiquated bathroom sink, wondering if he'd be able to fix the continual drip, drop, drip. From the looks of the nasty green stain, it had been leaking quite awhile. In a house this old, where little or no repairs had been done, Glen figured he'd be helping out for a good many weeks. He smiled to himself. It would mean more time spent with Sinda. Maybe he'd be able to find out what was bothering her, and why, if she was a Christian, she had no interest in church.

"Dad! Dad!" Tara rounded the corner of the bathroom and skidded to a stop next to him.

Glen knew right away that something was wrong—Tara's eyes were huge, and he felt her tremble as she clung to him. "What's wrong, Honey? You scared me half to death, screaming like that."

"You're scared?" she sobbed. "Go to that spooky basement by yourself, then you'll be scared!"

Glen pulled away slightly, so he could get a better look at her face. "What are you talking about?"

"Strange noises! Moving doll parts! I'm telling you, Dad, this house has to be haunted!"

Glen gave Tara's shoulders a gentle shake. "Take a deep breath and calm down."

"I heard a noise! A doll leg jumped out of a box! This place is creepy, and I want to go home." Tara's voice was pleading, and she squeezed Glen around the waist with a strength that surprised him. He wasn't sure how to deal with her hysteria and wondered if she might even be making the story up just to get him away from Sinda. He gritted his teeth. *If this is a ploy, she's not going to get away with it.*

⋙

Sinda entered the bathroom, but stopped short when she saw Tara clinging to her father. "I thought you were in the basement, Tara."

"She heard a noise." Glen shrugged his shoulders and looked

at Sinda with a helpless expression. "She thinks your house is haunted."

Tara seemed close to tears, and Sinda felt sorry for her. She was about to ask for an explanation, when Tara blurted, "A doll leg jumped right out of a box! I saw it with my own eyes."

Glen held up his hands. "What can I say?"

"I think I can take care of this little problem." Sinda started for the door.

"You're not going down there, are you?" Tara cried.

"Yes, I am. Me and Panther."

"Panther?" Glen and Tara said in unison.

"Panther's my new cat," Sinda explained as she started down the stairs.

Glen and Tara were right behind her. "I never knew you had a cat," Tara said. "You've got a dog, and cats and dogs don't usually get along."

Sinda nodded but kept descending the stairs. "You're right. Sparky's not the least bit fond of Panther, and I'm quite sure the cat returns his feelings. I try to keep them separated as much as possible." By now they were in the hallway, and Sinda began calling, "Here, kitty, kitty!"

"When did you get a cat?" Glen asked, moving toward Sinda.

"A few days ago. One of my customers is moving. She can't take Panther along, so I adopted him." She drew in a deep breath. "Since I'm having some trouble, I thought having a cat might be a good idea."

Glen slipped his arm around Sinda's waist, and she found the gesture comforting yet a bit disarming. "Trouble? What kind of trouble are you having?"

"I'll explain it all later," she said, moving away from Glen. "Right now I need to find that cat." Sinda stepped into the living room and called, "Panther! Come, kitty, kitty!"

Glen turned to Tara. "You're good with cats. Why don't you see if you can help?"

Tara shook her head and gave him an imploring look. "We need to get out of this house!"

"Tara Mae Olsen, would you quit being so melodramatic? Sinda needs our help, and it's the neighborly thing—"

Tara shook her head. "I just want to go home."

"We'll go as soon as we've helped Sinda solve her problem."

Sinda offered Glen a grateful smile. How could the man be so helpful and kind? Was it all an act, or did Glen Olsen really want to help?

twelve

A green-eyed ebony cat streaked through the living room with the speed of lightning. "That was Panther," Sinda announced.

"I sure hope he won't fight with Jake," Tara mumbled.

"You're fast on your feet, Tara. Go after him!" Glen pointed to the staircase where Panther had bounded.

Tara scrambled after the cat, and Glen followed Sinda to the kitchen. Five minutes later Tara came running in, holding tightly to the cat, its ears lying flat against its head in irritation.

Sinda had been sitting beside Glen at the table, drinking a cup of coffee, and just as he reached for her hand, Tara marched across the room and dropped Panther into her lap.

"You found him!" Sinda exclaimed. "Where was he?"

"Hiding inside a box in that room full of junk." Tara gave her ponytail a flip and scrunched up her nose.

Glen's forehead wrinkled as he looked at his daughter. "I hope you didn't disturb anything."

Tara flopped into a chair. "Nothing except the dumb old cat."

"Now that he's been found, let's put him to work." Sinda stood up and hurried to the basement door. Glen and Tara followed. She placed Panther on the first step and gave him a little nudge. "Go get 'em, boy!" Sinda slammed the door. "That should take care of our little basement ghosts."

"You're sending a cat to chase ghosts?" Tara's eyes were wide, and her mouth hung slightly open.

"Panther's on a mouse hunt," Sinda explained, moving back toward the kitchen.

Tara was right on her heels. "Mice? You think there are mice in the basement?"

Sinda nodded. "I told you that before. I think the jumping doll leg was a lively mouse who has taken up residence in the box of doll parts. You probably frightened him, and when he jumped, it caused the doll leg to go flying."

Glen nodded. "In an old house like this, it's not uncommon to find a few mice scurrying around. We don't want them over-running the place, though, so I think we should set some traps."

Sinda leaned against the cupboard. "That might help, but I'd rather let the cat take care of things naturally. I don't want to take the chance of either Sparky or Panther getting their noses caught in a trap."

"Or their tails," Tara added. Her gazed shifted to her father. "Remember when Jake got his tail caught in a mouse trap? That was awful!"

Glen held up his hands. "Okay, ladies. . .I get the point. We'll forget about setting any traps." He pulled Tara to his side and gave her a squeeze. "Guess what?"

She shrugged. "What?"

"Last Sunday, when Sinda came to our house for dinner, she invited us to eat at her place this Sunday." Glen smiled and winked at Sinda. "Now we get to try out some of her cooking."

Sinda was surprised Glen hadn't told his daughter about her dinner invitation until now, and the troubled look on Tara's face told Sinda all she needed to know. The child was not happy about this bit of news. *What have I done now?* she silently moaned.

❧

It had been raining all morning, and Sinda could see out the kitchen window where the water was running off the roof like it was being released from a dam. "We do need the rain, but now new gutters will have to be put up. Another job for poor, overworked Glen. Is there no end to the work needing to be done around this old place?" She groaned. "I can't believe I invited the Olsens over for dinner today." Tara didn't want to come, and when he'd phoned last night, Glen had once more tried to convince Sinda to go to church with them. As much as she enjoyed Glen's company, she couldn't go. The last time she'd gone to church. . .

Sinda turned away from the window and grabbed her recipe for scalloped potatoes from the cupboard. *I will not allow myself to think about the past today. Thinking about it won't change a thing, and it will only cause me more pain.* She wiped a stray hair away from her face and moaned. "Why don't children get to choose their parents? Life is so unfair."

Sinda heard a knock on the front door and hurried to the hall mirror to check her appearance. She was wearing her hair up in a French roll and had chosen to wear a beige, short-sleeved cotton dress that just touched her ankles. The prim and proper look was a far cry from her normal ponytail and cutoffs.

Sinda's hands trembled as she opened the door. Glen smiled and gave her an approving nod. "You look nice today." He was dressed in a pair of navy blue slacks and a light blue cotton shirt, which made his indigo eyes seem even more intense than usual. He handed Sinda a plate of chocolate chip cookies and a bouquet of miniature red roses.

"Thank you, they're lovely." She opened the door wider, bidding him entrance. "Where's Tara?"

"She'll be here soon. She couldn't decide whether to stay in her church clothes or change into something more comfortable."

"Why don't you put the cookies on the kitchen counter? I'll find a vase for these beauties and use them as our centerpiece. I bought some lemon sherbet the other day, so the cookies should go well with that." Sinda knew she was babbling, but she seemed unable to stop herself. *If Glen would only quit staring at me, I might not feel as nervous as a baby robin being chased by a cat.*

"What's for dinner?" Glen asked, lifting his dark eyebrows and sniffing the air. "Something smells pretty good."

"Nothing fancy. Just scalloped potatoes."

"I'm sure they'll be great." He cleared his throat a few times, as though he might be trying to work up the courage to say something more. "I–uh–have a question for you."

"What is it?" she asked as she filled the vase with water.

Glen moved slowly toward Sinda. Her mouth went dry, and

she swallowed so hard she almost choked. *What's he doing? I hope he's not...*

He took the vase from her hands and placed it on the counter. Then he pulled her into his arms. "My question is, how come you're so beautiful?"

Before Sinda could open her mouth to reply, his lips captured hers. The unexpected kiss left her weak in the knees and fighting for breath. When it ended, she pulled back slightly, gazing up at his handsome face. She pressed her head against his shoulder, breathing in the masculine scent of his subtle aftershave. She could feel the steady beat of Glen's heart against her ear, and she closed her eyes, feeling relaxed and safe in his embrace. Safer than she'd felt in a long time. What had happened to her resolve to keep her neighbor at arm's length? It was fading faster than a photograph left out in the sun, and she seemed powerless to stop it.

"I haven't felt this way about any woman since Connie died," Glen whispered. "I realize we haven't known each other very long, but I find myself thinking about you all the time." He lifted her chin with one hand, bent his head, and captured her mouth again.

How long the kiss might have lasted, Sinda would never know, for a shrill voice sliced through the air like a razor blade. "Dad, what are you doing?"

Glen pulled away first. He seemed almost in a daze as he stared at his daughter with a blank look on his face. Several awkward seconds ticked by, then he shook his head, as though coming out of a trance. "Tara, how'd you get here?"

"I walked. We live next door, remember?"

Glen's eyelids closed partway, and he shook his finger at Tara. "Don't get smart with me, young lady! I meant, why didn't you knock? You don't just walk into someone's house. I've taught you better manners than that."

Tara blinked several times, and Sinda wondered if the child was going to cry. "I did knock. Nobody answered, but since you were already here, I tried the door. It was open, so I thought it was okay to come in. Then I found you. . . ." Tara touched her lips with the tips of her fingers and grimaced. "That was really gross, Dad."

Sinda reached up with shaky fingers and brushed her own trembling lips. *What can I say or do to help ease this tension?*

Glen moved away from her and knelt in front of his daughter. "Sinda and I are both adults, and if we want to share a kiss, it shouldn't concern you."

Tara's eyes were wide, and she waved her hands in the air. "Why not? Dad, can't you see that Sinda's got you—"

Glen held up one hand. "That will be enough, Tara. I want you to apologize to Sinda for being so rude."

"It's okay." Sinda spoke softly, hoping to calm Glen down. From the angry scowl on his face, she was afraid he might be about to slap his daughter. She couldn't stand to witness such a scene, and she'd do almost anything to stop it from happening. Sinda touched Glen on the shoulder. "We didn't hear her knock, so she did the only thing she could think to do."

He stood up and put his arm around Sinda, but his gaze was fixed on Tara. "I'm glad Sinda is kind enough to forgive you, but you do need to apologize for your behavior," he said in a more subdued tone of voice.

Tara hung her head. "I–I'm sorry for coming into your house without being invited." She glanced up at Sinda, and tears shimmered in her dark eyes.

Sinda had the sudden urge to wrap the child in her arms and offer comfort, but she was sure it would not be appreciated. Tara obviously didn't like her, and she didn't think there was anything she could do to change that fact.

"I don't know about the rest of you, but I'm hungry," Glen said, changing the subject and breaking into Sinda's thoughts. "Is dinner ready yet?"

Sinda nodded. "I think so." She moved away from Glen and busied herself at the stove. *Inviting my neighbors to dinner was a terrible mistake, and it must never happen again.*

thirteen

"There's only one way to get Glen Olsen out of my mind," Sinda fumed, "and that's to keep busy."

She was alone in the doll hospital, working on an antique bisque doll. Panther, who was sleeping under the table, meowed softly, as though in response to her grumbling.

In spite of her determination not to think about Glen, Sinda's thoughts swirled around in her head like a blender running at full speed. It had been four weeks since she'd had Glen and Tara over for dinner, and during those four weeks she'd been miserable.

Sinda swallowed hard and fought the urge to give in to her tears. Glen had called her after he'd gone home that night, apologizing for Tara's behavior and suggesting that they try dinner the following Sunday at his place. When Sinda told him she didn't want to see him anymore, he seemed confused. She'd even said she didn't want him doing any more work on her house, and he had argued about that as well. Sinda knew having Glen around would be too much temptation, and she might weaken and agree to go out with him again. Or worse yet, let him kiss her again. Of course her decision meant she would either have to do all her own home repairs or pay someone else to do them. Until business picked up and she had a steady cash flow, she would forget about all repairs that weren't absolutely necessary.

Sinda could still hear Glen's final words before she'd hung up the phone that night. "I care about you, Sinda, and I really want to help."

She'd almost weakened, but an image of her mother had jumped into her mind. There was no future for her and Glen, so why lead him on? And even if her past wasn't working against her, Tara certainly was!

The telephone rang, and Sinda's mind snapped back to the present. She reached for it, thankful that she'd remembered to bring the cordless phone downstairs this time. "Sinda's Doll Hospital." Her eyebrows shot up. "You want to run a story about me in your newspaper? I–I–guess it would be all right. Yes, I'd like it to be a human interest story too." *That would no doubt be good for my business.*

Several minutes later she hung up the phone, having agreed to let a reporter from the *Daily Herald* interview her the following morning. She hoped it was the right decision.

ð

The interview with the newspaper columnist went better than Sinda had expected, but she was relieved when he and his photographer said they had all they needed and left her house shortly before noon. Even though she knew the article they planned to print about her doll hospital would be good for business, Sinda had some reservations about having so much attention drawn to her. She'd always tried to stay out of the limelight, and during her childhood none of her friends except Carol had been invited to her home. Carol had only come over a few times, and that was always whenever Sinda's father was gone.

Thinking about her friend reminded Sinda that Carol had promised to come over after work today and help her paint the kitchen cabinets. After lunch she would go to the nearest hardware store and buy some paint.

Sinda knew Glen probably could paint the cabinets much faster and probably a whole lot neater than she or Carol, but she couldn't ask for his help. . .not after his daughter had seen them kissing and thrown such a fit. No matter how much it pained her, she had to keep her distance.

ð

Glen paced back and forth in front of the counter at the hardware store, waiting for his brother to finish with a customer. He'd been promising himself for the last several weeks to repaint the barbecue and had decided to stop by Phil's Hardware on the way home from work and pick up what he needed for the project. He hoped to have several barbecues this summer and was getting a late start. *Too bad they won't include Sinda Shull,* he fumed inwardly. *I know the woman likes me, and she's just being stubborn, refusing to see me or even let me continue with the repairs on her home. If only there were some way I could convince her that my jealous daughter will eventually come around. I know Sinda has some issues she needs to resolve, but that's even more reason I should keep seeing her. I might be able to help.*

"Hey, big brother, it's good to see you!"

Glen turned toward Phil, who was finally finished with his customer. He grabbed his brother in a bear hug. "It's good to see you too. It's been awhile, huh?"

Phil swiped a hand across his bearded chin and frowned. "I'll say. Where have you been keeping yourself, anyway?"

Glen was tempted to tell Phil about his new neighbor, and that up until a few weeks ago, he'd been helping Sinda with some repairs on her rambling old house, but he thought better of it. Phil was a confirmed bachelor, and whenever he discovered that Glen had dated any woman, Phil bombarded him with a bunch of wisecracks and unwanted advice.

"I've been busy." Glen nodded at Phil. "What's new in your life?"

Phil shrugged, and his blue eyes twinkled. "Until a few minutes ago, nothing was new."

Glen's interest was piqued. "What's that supposed to mean?"

"I've met the woman of my dreams," Phil said, running his fingers through his curly black hair. "She came in awhile ago, looking for some paint, and it was love at first sight."

Glen chuckled. How many times had he heard his goofy brother say he'd found the perfect woman, only to drop her flat when he became bored? Glen was sure this latest attraction would be no different than the others had been.

"You're not going to say anything?" Phil asked expectantly.

Glen shrugged his shoulders. "What would you like me to say?"

Phil wiggled his dark, bushy eyebrows, and Glen had a vision of his kid brother as an enormous teddy bear. "How about, 'Wow, brother, that's great. When do I get to meet this woman of your dreams?' "

"Okay, okay," Glen said, laughing. "When do I get to meet her?"

Phil turned his hands palm up. "Maybe you already have. She's your next-door neighbor."

Glen felt his jaw drop. "Sinda Shull?"

Phil nodded. "Like I said, she came in looking for some paint for her kitchen, and we got to talking. She told me she wants a new screen for her back door, and since the size she needs is out of stock, I promised to order one today and deliver it to her house as soon as it comes in." He smiled triumphantly. "That's how I got her address and discovered she lives next door to you. Small world, isn't it?"

"Too small if you ask me," Glen mumbled as he moved toward the front door.

"Hey, where are you going?"

"Home. Tara's probably starving, and I need to get dinner started."

"But you never said what you came in for."

Glen hunched his shoulders and offered his brother a half-hearted wave. "I came by for some heat-resistant paint, but it can wait. See you later, Phil." He left the hardware store feeling like someone had punched him in the stomach. Not only had Sinda decided to do some painting without his help, but she'd gone to his brother's store to buy the paint. As if that wasn't bad enough, Phil suddenly had a big crush on a woman he didn't even know, and he was obviously looking forward to delivering Sinda's new screen door. Glen loved his little brother, but he cared too much for Sinda to let her be taken in by Phil the Pill. He would do whatever it took to prevent her from being hurt. Trouble was, with her refusing to see him, he didn't have a clue what he could do other than pray. "That's it," he muttered under his breath. "I'll pray for answers until they come."

❧

Tara let out a low whistle. "Wow! Take a look at this, Dad!"

"What is it?" Glen asked as he continued to chop mushrooms for the omelet he was making.

"Our weirdo neighbor lady made the newspaper. Listen to what it says: 'Doll Doctor Has Heavy Caseload.' " Tara stifled a giggle behind the paper. "Pretty impressive, huh?"

Glen wiped his hands on a paper towel and sauntered over to the kitchen table. "Let me see that." He snatched the newspaper out of Tara's hands. "I want you to stop referring to Sinda as 'our weirdo neighbor lady.' She's not weird!" He was still upset over the conversation he'd had with Phil the day before, and he didn't need anything else to get riled about.

Tara shook her head. "She plays with dolls, Dad. Don't you think that's kinda weird?"

"No, I don't, and how many times must I remind you what the Bible says about loving our neighbor?"

Tara shrugged. "I know, but—"

"Sinda is kind, sensitive, and reserved." Glen frowned. "And she doesn't play with dolls; she repairs them." His eyes quickly scanned the article about Sinda Shull who'd recently opened a doll hospital in the basement of her home. The story went on to say that almost any doll, no matter how old or badly damaged, could be repaired by an expert such as Doll Doctor Shull. There was a picture of Sinda sitting at her workbench, sanding a wooden doll head.

"She looks great," Glen murmured.

Tara groaned. "Where's Sinda been lately? I haven't seen her since I finished my punishment in her creepy basement. She hasn't been around making eyes at you, and it makes me wonder what's up."

Methodically, Glen pulled on his left earlobe. He knew exactly how long it had been since he'd last talked to Sinda.

He'd seen her a few times out in the yard, but whenever he tried to make conversation, she always concocted some lame excuse to go back inside. Just when he and Sinda seemed to be getting closer, she'd pulled away. He didn't like this hot and cold stuff. *Well, maybe it's for the best. Even though Sinda says she's a Christian, she doesn't want anything to do with church. It might be better for all concerned if I bow out graciously.*

He shook his head, hoping to clear away the troubling thoughts. Who was he kidding? He didn't want to let Sinda walk out of his life. She was afraid of something, and it was probably more than concern over Tara's reaction to their relationship. Besides, he had to protect Sinda from his little brother. Phil might look like a teddy bear but he acted more like a grizzly bear.

"Dad, are you listening to me?"

Glen lifted both elbows and flexed his shoulders as he stretched, then dropped the newspaper to the table. "What were you saying?"

"I asked about Sinda. Why do you think she hasn't been around lately?"

"I'm sure she's been busy." He pointed to the newspaper. "That article even says so."

"I guess a lot of people have broken dolls, huh?"

Glen gave a noncommittal grunt, thinking of the doll he'd given Sinda to repair. He wondered if she would still make good on it, even though she'd changed her mind and wouldn't allow him to do any more repairs on her house. If she did finish repairing it, he would gladly pay her whatever it cost.

"I'm sure happy I don't have to help in that doll hospital anymore." Tara looked at him pointedly. "It was awful!"

"I thought you liked fixing broken dolls."

"It was okay at first, but that house is creepy and full of strange noises. Besides, I don't like Sinda. She's w—I mean, different."

"God created each of us differently," Glen said patiently. "The world would be a boring place if we were all alike."

Tara scrunched up her nose. "Sinda is way different."

"Are you sure you aren't jealous?" Glen asked, taking a seat at the table.

"Why would I be?"

He raised his eyebrows. "Maybe you're envious of the attention I've shown Sinda."

"You can't help yourself because she's got you hypnotized with those green cat's eyes."

"Don't start with that again."

Tara held up both hands. "Okay, okay. I'm just glad Sinda hasn't been hanging around. I'm happy you're not going over there anymore, either."

"It's your fault I'm not," Glen blurted without thinking.

Tara flinched, making him feel like a rotten father. "What do you mean, it's my fault?"

"One of the reasons—probably the main one—Sinda won't see me anymore, is because she thinks you don't like her."

"She's right about that," Tara muttered. "I'm glad she's not around anymore."

"Tara Mae Olsen, that's an awful thing to say!" He leveled her with a look he hoped would make her realize the seriousness of the situation. "In the book of Proverbs we are told that he who despises his neighbor, sins."

"I don't despise Sinda, Dad. It's just that I know she's after you." Tara grabbed hold of his shirtsleeve. "She's trying to win you over with compliments and flirty looks."

"Flirty looks? What would a little girl know about flirty looks?"

She grinned at him. "I'm not a baby, you know."

Glen smiled, in spite of his irritation. "That's right, you're not." He patted the top of her head. "So try not to act like one."

fourteen

As Glen knelt on the patio to begin scraping the rusted paint off his barbecue, he heard a noisy vehicle pull into Sinda's driveway. He straightened, rubbed the kinks out of his back, and moved casually around the side of the house. He didn't want to be seen or have anyone get the idea he was spying, so he crouched down by his front porch and peeked into Sinda's yard. It was just as he feared. . .a truck bearing the name "Phil's Hardware" was parked in her driveway, and Phil the Pill was climbing down from the driver's seat. Glen watched as his brother went around to the back of the pickup and withdrew a screen door. He whistled as he walked toward Sinda's front door, and it was all Glen could do to keep from jumping up, dashing through the gate, and grabbing Phil by the shirttail.

That would be ridiculous, Glen reprimanded himself. *It's a free country, and my brother's only doing his job. If Sinda ordered the screen door, Phil has every right to deliver it.*

"Why don't you use my binoculars, Dad?"

Glen whirled around at the sound of his daughter's voice. "Tara, you scared me! Why are you sneaking up on me like that?"

Tara snickered. "It looks like you were spying on someone." She shook her head and clicked her tongue. "Is it Sinda?"

Glen stood up straight and faced his daughter. "I wasn't spying on Sinda."

"Who then?"

"Uncle Phil."

Tara's forehead wrinkled. "Huh?"

Glen took Tara by the arm and led her around back, so they wouldn't be overheard. "I heard a vehicle pull into Sinda's driveway, and I thought I recognized the sound of Uncle Phil's truck. So, I went around front to check it out, and sure enough, he's delivering a new screen door to Sinda."

"That's good. Her old one was about to fall."

Glen opened his mouth to comment, but Tara cut him off. "Why don't we go over and tell Uncle Phil hello? We haven't seen him in ages."

He smiled. For once Tara had a good idea, and since this was her idea, Glen had a legitimate excuse to see Sinda.

❧

Sinda came upstairs at the sound of a truck in her driveway, then peeked out the living room window. "Ah, my screen door has arrived." She hurried to open the front door, and Phil from Phil's Hardware met her on the porch. He leaned the screen door against the side of the house and grinned. "Where do you want this beauty?"

"Around back, please."

Phil hoisted it again like it weighed no more than a feather and stepped off the porch. Sinda followed.

"You got anyone lined up to install this?" Phil asked when they reached the backyard.

Install it? Sinda hadn't even thought about how she would replace her old screen with the new one. She gnawed on her lower lip as she contemplated the problem. "I guess I could try to put it up myself." Even as the words slipped off her tongue, Sinda realized it was a bad idea. She knew as much about putting up a screen door as a child understood the mechanics of driving a car.

"I'd be happy to install it for you," Phil offered as he set it down, leaning it against the porch railing. "In fact, I've got my helper working at the store all afternoon, so I could do it now if you like."

"How much would you charge?"

Phil shrugged his broad shoulders and gave her a lopsided grin. "Tell you what, I'll put up the door while I work up the nerve to ask you out to dinner."

Sinda swallowed hard. "Dinner?"

"Yeah, maybe some beer and pizza. I know this great place—"

She held up her hand. "I don't drink alcoholic beverages. I also don't go out with men I hardly know." *Except Glen Olsen,* her conscience reminded. *You went out with Glen a few weeks after you met.*

Phil took a step toward Sinda. "We introduced ourselves when you came into my store the other day, and sharing dinner would give us a chance to get better acquainted." He winked at her, and she was about to reply when Glen and Tara came bounding into the yard.

"Hey, Brother, I heard the unmistakable rumble of your truck and thought I'd come over and say hi." Glen gave Phil a hearty slap on the back, then he turned to face Sinda.

She eyed him curiously. "You and Phil are brothers?" Except for the dark hair and blue eyes, the two men didn't look anything alike. Glen was slender and clean-shaven while Phil was stocky and sported a full beard. He also had a cocky attitude, which was the total opposite of Glen.

Before Glen could answer Sinda's question, Tara spoke up. "Uncle Phil's Dad's little brother." She looked up at her uncle and gave his loose shirttail a good yank. "How come you haven't been over to see us in such a long time?"

"Guess I've been too busy to socialize," Phil said, tugging on Tara's ponytail in response. His gaze swung back to Sinda, and he gave her another flirtatious wink. "I'm hoping to remedy that now that I've met your beautiful new neighbor." He glanced at his brother, and Sinda noticed that Glen wasn't smiling. In fact, he looked downright irritated.

"I plan to install Sinda's new screen door, then she's going out to dinner with me," Phil remarked with a smirk.

Sinda opened her mouth, but she never got a word out. "Is that so?" Glen interrupted. "Don't you have a store to run?"

Phil tucked his thumbs inside his jeans pockets and rocked back and forth on his heels. "Gabe's workin' for me all day, so I can spare a few minutes to put up Sinda's door." He reached out and grabbed hold of the screen, still leaning against the porch railing.

Before he could take a step, Glen seized the door and jerked it right out of Phil's hands. "Sinda hired me to do some repairs on her house in exchange for—" Glen paused and glanced down at his daughter. "Uh, I mean—I agreed to help her out, so putting up the screen door is my job."

Phil looked at Sinda, then back at Glen. "She said she had nobody to install the screen, and I volunteered."

"Is that a fact?"

Phil nodded and reached for the screen door.

Sinda wasn't sure what she should do or say. Glen and Phil were arguing over who would complete the task, but she had a feeling the tug-of-war had more to do with her than it did the door. She'd never had two men fight for her attention before, and it was a bit unnerving.

"I've got an idea," Tara interjected. "Dad, why don't you and Uncle Phil both put Sinda's screen door up? That way the job will get done twice as fast."

Glen shrugged. "I guess we could do that."

Phil nodded. "You know what they say—four hands are better than two."

"I think that's 'two heads are better than one,' Uncle Phil." Tara giggled and jabbed her uncle in the ribs.

He chortled. "Yeah, whatever."

A thought popped into Sinda's head, and she wondered why the idea hadn't come to her sooner. "I'll appreciate the help no matter who sets the screen door in place, but I won't be going out with anyone. I've got some work to do. So if you men will excuse me, I'm going downstairs to my workshop." With that, she stepped into the house and closed the door.

❧

It was another warm Saturday, and Glen was outside mowing his lawn. He waved at Tara, who was across the street visiting her friend Penny, then he stopped to fill the mower with gas. A bloodcurdling scream, which sounded like it had come from Sinda's house, halted his actions.

Sinda's terrier, Sparky, was yapping through the fence, and Glen turned his head in that direction. Maybe Sinda had come face-to-face with an intruder. She might be hurt and in need of his help. *Maybe that goofy brother of mine is back, and he's bugging Sinda to go out with him again.*

With no further thought, Glen tore open the gate and raced into Sinda's backyard, nearly tripping over the black dog. There was another shrill scream, and Glen was sure it was coming from Sinda's basement. He made a dash for the door and gave the handle a firm yank. It didn't budge. "Must be locked," he muttered. He pounded on the door, calling out Sinda's name.

The door flew open, and Sinda threw herself into his arms. Glen felt like his heart had jumped right into his throat. Something was terribly wrong. "What is it? What happened down here?"

"I think Tara may be right about this spooky old house being haunted," she said with a deep moan.

Glen held her at arm's length as he studied her tear-streaked face. Sinda's deadpan expression and quivering lower lip told him how serious she was. *At least my bear of a brother wasn't the reason for her panic.* "Tell me what happened," he said as he took hold of her trembling hand.

She hiccuped. "A doll head. I saw a doll head."

"You screamed loud enough to wake a sleeping hound dog, and you're telling me it was just a doll head that scared you?" Glen knew women were prone to hysterics, but this was ridiculous.

"It was in my freezer," Sinda whimpered. "I found a vinyl doll head in the freezer."

Glen stood there several seconds, trying to digest this strange piece of information. He could understand what a shock it would be to open the freezer, fully intending to retrieve a package of meat, and discover a doll head staring back at him instead. "Someone's probably playing a trick on you." Glen's thoughts went immediately to his daughter, even though Tara hadn't been working in Sinda's doll hospital for several weeks. Unless she planted it there on her last day. "How long has it been since you opened the freezer?"

She shrugged. "A week—maybe two."

"Are you sure? It hasn't been any longer?"

"I think I took some ice cream out last Saturday." She nodded and swiped her hand across her chin. "Yes, that's the last time I opened it."

"And there was no doll head then?"

"I'm sure there wasn't."

A feeling of relief washed over Glen. He didn't see how it could have been Tara. He led Sinda into the basement. "Is the doll head still in the freezer?"

"Yes. When I first saw it, I screamed and slammed the door. Then I thought I must have been seeing things, so I opened the freezer again, but it was still there." She leaned heavily against him and drew in a shuddering breath. "I heard someone pounding on the basement door, and when I opened it and saw you, I kind of fell apart."

And right into my arms, Glen thought with a wry smile. At least something good came out of this whole weird experience. "Why don't you show me the doll?" he suggested.

Sinda gripped Glen's hand tightly as she led the way to the utility room. "Would you mind opening the freezer? I don't think I have the strength."

Glen grasped the handle and jerked the freezer door open. A round head with brown painted hair and bright blue eyes stared back at him. It was so creepy he almost let out a yelp himself. He reached inside to remove the icy-cold doll head. "Looks a little chilly, doesn't it?"

"I've been looking everywhere for that!" Sinda exclaimed. "It and several other doll parts have been missing for a few weeks."

Glen scratched the back of his head. "Hmm. . .sounds like a bit of a mystery to me. Maybe we should put Detective Tara

Mae Olsen on the case. She'd love something as weird as this to sink her teeth into."

Sinda was obviously not amused by his comment. She was scared to death, and it showed clearly on her ashen face. Glen placed the doll head on top of the dryer and drew her into his arms. It felt so right to hold her like this. Too bad she didn't realize how good they could be for each other.

"Glen—"

"Sinda—"

Glen chuckled. "Go ahead."

"No, you first."

"I know there has to be a simple answer to this whole thing."

She looked up at him expectantly. "What could it be?"

He shrugged. "I don't know. Do you think you could have accidentally put the head into the freezer? I've done some pretty strange things when I'm preoccupied." He grinned. "Like putting dishwasher soap in the refrigerator instead of the cupboard."

She gave him a weak smile. "I know everyone is absent-minded at times, but I don't even remember picking the doll head up, much less putting it in the freezer. Besides, what about the other missing doll parts?"

Glen frowned. "Maybe you misplaced them. I do that with my car keys a lot."

"You think I'm getting forgetful in my old age?"

"Hardly," he said with a wink. "Seriously, though, even if I'm not sure what's going on with the doll parts, I don't want anything to happen to our friendship." He brushed her cheek with the back of his hand. "I know you said you didn't want to see me anymore, but I'm hoping you'll reconsider. Please don't let Tara's resistance be a deciding factor."

Sinda licked her lips. "I want to see you, Glen, but it's not a good idea."

"Why not?"

"There are things in my past that prevent me from making a commitment to you—or any other man."

His eyebrows arched. "Are you trying to tell me that you lied about not being married?"

"No, of course not! I'm as single as any woman could be."

"And you're a Christian?"

Sinda nodded. "I am, but—"

"Then what's the problem?" Glen's finger curved under her trembling chin, and she met his gaze with a look that went straight to his heart. He felt as if her pain was his, and he wondered what he could do to help ease her discomfort. Instinctively, he bent his head to kiss her. When they broke away, he whispered, "I don't care about your past, Sinda. If you're a Christian, and you care for me, that's all that counts. We can work through any problems you have from your past." He kissed the tip of her nose. "No matter what you say, I'm not giving up on you. So there!"

fifteen

"Where do we go from here?" Sinda asked Glen as she took a chair directly across from him.

Glen rapped his knuckles on the kitchen table and looked thoughtful. "I want to get to the bottom of the missing doll parts, but first I think we need to figure out some way to get our relationship back on track."

"I let you put up my screen door," she reminded.

"I'm talking about our personal relationship."

A film of tears obscured her vision. "But, Glen—"

He held up one hand. "I know. You have secrets from your past and can't make any kind of commitment."

She nodded in response and clasped her hands around her knees to keep them from shaking.

"We all have things from our past that we'd like to forget," he said softly. "But God doesn't want us to dwell on the past. So why don't we pray about this, then we'll deal with one problem at a time." He paused and flicked a crumb off the table. "I think it might help to talk about what's troubling you before we pray."

She counted on her fingers. "Lost doll parts. . .a vinyl head in the freezer. . .how's that for starters?"

He nodded. "We'll take care of that in good time, but right now we need to deal with the reason you won't allow me into your life."

Sinda wiped away the unwanted tears she felt on her cheeks and avoided his gaze. Silence wove around her, filling up the space between them. "I–I haven't dated much, and I've never been in love. Even the thought of it scares me." She swallowed hard. "I'm not sure I could ever love a man, so there's no point in leading you on."

"What are you afraid of, Sinda?"

"I'm afraid of love. I'm afraid of being hurt."

Glen's thumb stroked the top of her hand, and her skin tingled with each feathery touch. "Who are you angry with?" he coaxed.

Sinda jerked her hand away. Glen was treading on dangerous territory now. "What makes you think I'm angry?"

He leaned forward and studied her intently. "It's written all over your face. I hear it in the tone of your voice."

"Your daughter thinks she's a detective, and now you're moonlighting as a psychologist," she said sarcastically.

"I'm only trying to help, but I can't if you won't let me."

Sinda's nerves were tight like a rubber band. Angry, troubled thoughts tumbled around in her head, and she stared off into space. She wanted to run, to hide, and never have to deal with her pain. "My mother! I'm angry with my mother!" Sinda's hand went instinctively to her mouth. She hadn't meant to say that. It wasn't for Glen to know.

Glen seemed unaffected by her outrage. "What did your mother do?" he prompted.

Sinda sniffed deeply. She'd already let the cat out of the bag, so she may as well get the rest off her chest. "She left my father when I was ten years old."

"Left him? You mean she died?"

Sinda shook her head, swallowing back the pain and humiliation. "She walked out."

"Was there another man involved?"

A shuddering sigh escaped Sinda's trembling lips, and she was powerless to stop it. "No!" She gulped in a deep breath. "At least, I don't think so. She left us a note, but it didn't explain her reason for abandoning us. Her message said only that she was going and would never come back. There was no other explanation—not even an apology." Sinda picked at an imaginary piece of fuzz on her peach-colored T-shirt. "Mother was there when I went to bed one night, and she was gone the next morning when I awoke."

Glen reached for her hand again, and this time she didn't pull away. "I'm so sorry, Sinda."

"My father was devastated by her betrayal, and he. . ." Her voice trailed off. How could she explain about Dad? She'd never fully understood him herself.

"I'm sure it must have been hard on both you and your father," Glen acknowledged. "If you're ready, I'd like to pray now, then we can talk some more."

She shrugged. "I–I guess so."

With her hand held firmly in his, Sinda bowed her head. "Dear Lord," Glen prayed, "Sinda has some pain from her past that needs to be healed. We know You are the Great Physician and it's within Your power to heal physically and emotionally. Please touch Sinda's heart and let her feel Your presence. Help us get to the bottom of the missing doll parts, and we thank You in advance for Your answers. Amen."

When Sinda opened her eyes, she was able to offer Glen a brief smile. She felt a bit better after his beseeching prayer. It was a relief to have him know some of her past, and it was comforting to sit with him here in her kitchen. "Whenever anyone asks about Mother, I sort of leave the impression that she died," she said with a shrug of her shoulders. "To me she is dead. I hate what she did to Dad."

"To your dad?" Glen exclaimed. "What about what she did to you? Have you ever dealt with that?"

Sinda shook her head. "I try not to think about it. Dad was all I had, and until he died, I devoted my whole life to him." She gulped and tried to regain her composure. "I hadn't thought about Mother in years. Not until that stupid trunk arrived. It was hers, but I thought Dad threw it out after she left."

"Have you looked through it yet? It might help heal some of your pain."

Sinda jumped up and began pacing the floor. "I still can't find a key that fits the lock. My lawyer said Dad wanted me to have the trunk, but he didn't give him a key."

"I'm sure the lock can be broken. I'd be happy to do it for you," Glen offered.

Sinda stopped pacing and turned to face him. "I'm not sure I want to look at her things. I've spent most of my life trying to forget my mother. She wanted out of our lives and never made any effort to contact us, so why should I care about anything that belonged to her?"

"I'll stay with you. We can deal with this together."

"What about the missing doll parts?" Sinda grasped the back of a chair and grimaced. "I thought we were going to get to the bottom of that problem."

He nodded. "We are, but right now I think you should look through the trunk."

She held up her hands in defeat. "Okay, let's get this over with."

ہ

Sinda clicked on the overhead light in the storage room upstairs, and the bulky trunk came into view. She couldn't believe she'd actually told Glen the story of how Mother had abandoned her and Dad. It was a secret she'd promised never to share with anyone. Even her best friend Carol didn't know the truth. *Glen Olsen must have a powerful effect on me.*

Glen knelt beside the trunk and studied the lock. "I'd better go home and get a hacksaw." He glanced up at Sinda. "Unless you have one."

She shook her head. "I don't think so. After Dad died, I sold most of his tools. All I kept were the basics—a hammer, screwdriver, and a few other small items."

"Okay. I'll be back in a flash." Glen stood up. Her face lifted to meet his gaze, and she wanted to melt in the warmth of his sapphire blue eyes. "If you're nervous about being here alone, you're welcome to come along," he said, giving her shoulder a gentle squeeze.

"I'll be okay—as long as I stay away from the basement."

Glen dropped a kiss to her forehead, then he was gone. She stared down at the trunk and, giving her thoughts free reign, an image of her mother came to mind. Sinda closed her eyes, trying to shut out the vision, but her mother's face, so much like her own, was as clear as the antique crystal vase sitting on her fireplace mantel.

"You did this to me, Mother," Sinda sobbed. "Why couldn't you let the past stay in the past?" She trembled. Was there something wrong with her? Hadn't Dad accused her of being just like Mother? Hadn't he told her that if she didn't exercise control over her emotions, she'd end up hurting some poor unsuspecting man, the way Mother had hurt him?

In spite of the pain he'd often inflicted upon her, Sinda's heart ached for her dad. He'd been the victim of his wife's abandonment. Marla Shull had given no thought to anyone but herself, leaving him to care for their only child. *What a heartless thing to do,* Sinda thought bitterly. *Mother couldn't have felt any love for me, or you either, Dad. You don't walk out on someone you love.*

Sinda leaned over and fingered the lock on the trunk. "You made Dad the way he was, Mother, and I'm the one who suffered for it." *If only I hadn't been so much like you. If only. . .*

The prayer Glen prayed earlier replayed itself in her mind. It seemed like a genuine prayer—a plea to God for help. Dad's prayers always seemed genuine too—at least those he prayed at church meetings.

Sinda thought about the last time she'd gone to church. It was the night before Dad's heart attack, and they'd gone to a revival service. She would never forget the sight of her father kneeling at the altar during the close of the meeting. Had it been for show, like all the other times, or was Dad truly repentant for his sins?

Her mind took her back to the evening before the revival, when she and Dad had argued about the steak she'd fixed for dinner. He said it was overly done, and she'd tried to explain that the oven was too hot and needed repairing. She could still see the hostility on Dad's face when his hand connected to the side of her head. She could feel the pain and humiliation as she rushed to her room in tears.

That night at church, with Dad lying prostrate before the wooden altar, Sinda had been convinced that his display of emotions was only for attention, and at that moment, she vowed never to step inside another church. There were hypocrites there, and even those who weren't didn't seem able to discern when someone was physically and emotionally abusing their daughter. Whenever Dad walked into the sanctuary, he put on his "Mr. Christian" mask, but it fell off the moment they returned home.

Sinda hated her father's cruel treatment and hypocrisy at church, but she hated herself even more. After all, it was because she reminded him so much of her mother that Dad treated her the way he did.

Glen entered the room again, carrying a small hacksaw, and Sinda was thankful for the interruption. She'd spent enough time reliving the past and its painful memories.

"It's time to go to work," Glen announced. He knelt beside the trunk and quickly put the saw to good use. A few minutes later the lock snapped in two and fell to the floor with a thud.

Sinda took a deep breath to steady her nerves, and Glen moved aside. "You can open it now."

She knelt in front of the trunk, grasped the handle, and slowly opened the lid. There were a few items of clothing on top—a faded bridal veil, several lace handkerchiefs, and a delicate satin christening gown with a matching bonnet. Sinda fingered the soft material, remembering pictures that proved it had been her own. She moved the clothes aside and continued to explore.

"Would you rather be alone?" Glen asked, offering her a sympathetic smile.

She gazed at him through her pain and confusion. "No, please stay. I need the moral support."

He reached out and touched her arm. "I'll be here as long as you need me."

There was a small, green velvet box underneath the clothes.

Sinda opened it, revealing several pieces of jewelry she recognized as her mother's. She placed the jewelry box and the clothes on a chair, then carried on with her search through the trunk. A few seconds later, she pulled out an old photo album. "There's probably a lot of pictures in here, and I'd like to look at them. Maybe we should go downstairs where it's more comfortable."

Glen shrugged. "Tara's spending the day with her friend across the street, so you've got me all to yourself."

"Let's go to the living room." She stood, then moved quickly toward the door.

They sat on the couch for over an hour, going through the album and talking about Sinda's childhood before her mother walked out.

"Your mother was a beautiful woman," Glen remarked. "You look a lot like her."

"I do have her green eyes and auburn hair," Sinda agreed. She drew in a deep breath and let it out in a rush. "Dad used to say I had her personality too."

"I'm sure he meant it as a compliment."

Sinda snapped the album shut, nearly catching his fingers inside. "He didn't mean it that way at all! He meant it as a warning. He used to tell me that if I wasn't careful, I'd end up wrecking some poor man's life the way Mother ruined his."

"You didn't believe him, I hope."

She bit down hard on her bottom lip, until she tasted blood. "I had no reason not to."

Glen took her hand and gave it a gentle squeeze. "Who can discern his errors? Forgive my hidden faults," he said softly.

She tipped her head to one side. "What?"

"It's a quote from the book of Psalms," he explained, "and it means—"

"Never mind," she said, cutting him off. She placed the album on the coffee table and stood up. "I've had enough reminiscing for one day. I'd really like to look for those missing doll parts."

"Let's start in the basement," Glen suggested.

She was glad he hadn't kept prying into her past. There was too much pain there to deal with right now.

Glen led the way, and when they reached their destination, Sinda turned on a light in the room where she worked. "As you can see," she said, motioning with her hand, "I keep the dolls that come in for repairs on the shelf marked Emergency Room."

Glen whistled. "Pretty impressive!"

"I use the wooden table in the center of the room to do the work, then when a doll is done, I place it over there." She pointed to a shelf labeled Recovery Room.

"What about the parts and supplies you use for repairing? Where do you keep those?"

"Right there." She indicated another row of shelves on the opposite wall.

Glen nodded. "Are the missing pieces from a particular doll patient or from your supply of parts?"

"From my supply. Why do you ask?"

"Isn't it possible that you've already used the missing parts to repair some doll? Maybe you forgot which ones you used and thought they were still in a box. It could be that they're not really missing at all."

"There's just one flaw in your theory, Glen."

"What's that?"

"I keep good track of my inventory. To have three or four different parts missing at the same time doesn't add up."

Glen shrugged his shoulders. "It was only an idea."

"And let's not forget about that doll head in the freezer," Sinda reminded.

"How could I? It even gave me the creeps." He clapped his hands together. "Let's get to work. Those parts have to be down here someplace."

sixteen

The search for the missing doll parts turned up nothing. Glen was a bit frustrated, but Sinda seemed to be filled with despair. They'd given up for the day and left the basement for the comfort of her living room, and now Glen sat on the couch with his arm draped across her shoulders. "I'm sorry we didn't find anything. I can't figure it out."

Sinda lifted her head slightly and looked at him. "It's not your fault."

"We still have no doll parts, and from the way you're looking at me, I'd say I haven't done much to help alleviate your fears."

"Just having you here has helped."

They sat in silence for awhile, then Glen came up with a plan. "Since being down in the basement makes you so uptight, why not let me come over and give you a hand?"

Her forehead wrinkled. "Doing what?"

"Repairing dolls. I'm sure there's something I can do to help."

"Are you teasing me?"

He saw the skepticism in her squinted eyes and shook his head. "Who knows, it might even prove to be kind of fun."

"Oh, Glen," Sinda said shakily, "that's such a sweet offer, but—"

"I can come over every evening for a few hours, and on the Saturdays I'm not on my mail route."

"I couldn't let you do that."

"Why not? Are you afraid I'll make your doll patients even sicker?" he asked with a grin.

"It's not that. I'm sure you'd do fine, but you've got your own life. You have responsibilities to your daughter."

"Maybe Tara could tag along," he suggested.

"You two have better things to do than repair dolls and hold my shaking hand. Just because I'm acting like a big chicken doesn't mean you have to baby-sit me." Sinda paused as she slid her tongue across her lower lip. "Besides, you can't always be down there with me."

"Why not? I'd gladly spend my free time helping if it would make you feel better."

"I go to the basement for lots of things that don't involve doll repairing," she reminded him. "My washer and dryer are down there, and so is my freezer."

Glen lifted Sinda's chin with his thumb. "I think I'm falling in love with you, and I believe God brought you to Elmwood for a purpose," he said, changing the subject.

She opened her mouth to say something, but he touched her lips with the tips of his fingers and whispered, "If we give this relationship a chance, we might even have a future together."

Sinda sat up straight, her back rigid, and her lips set in a thin line. "We can't have a future together, Glen. I can't love you."

"Can't, or won't?"

She averted his steady gaze. "I want to love you, but I can't. My life is all mixed up, and my past would always be in our way. Please don't pressure me."

The depth of sadness he saw reflected in her green eyes made his stomach clench, and he nodded in mock defeat. "I'll drop the subject." *For now, anyway.*

❧

It had been three days since Sinda found the doll head in the freezer, and three days since Glen had declared his feelings for her. He'd phoned several times, and he'd come over twice to see how was she doing. She'd assured him that everything was fine, but it was a lie. How could anything be fine when she had doll parts unaccounted for and love burning in her heart for a man with whom she could never have a future?

Sinda had only been to the basement twice in the last three

days. Once to retrieve clothes from the dryer, and another time to bring up a doll that needed some work. She planned to put the finishing touches on the painted face while working at her kitchen table. She knew she couldn't keep it up forever, but for now, until her nerves settled down, she'd do more of the doll repairs upstairs, only going to the basement to get necessary items or do laundry.

A Girl Scout leader had called yesterday, wanting to bring her troop to the doll hospital as a field trip. Sinda turned her down, saying she was too busy right now. The truth was, the idea of having a bunch of inquisitive girls roaming around her basement would have been too much to handle.

In spite of Sinda's emotional state, she had managed to go to a local swap meet this morning where she'd sold a few antiques and picked up some old doll parts. She'd even met with two new customers who wanted dolls restored before Christmas.

Her chores were done for the day now, and she stood in the spare bedroom, prepared to check out the rest of the contents of her mother's trunk. She glanced around the room. Everything was exactly as she'd left it on Saturday. The jewelry box and items of clothing were still on the chair. The trunk lid was closed, though no longer locked.

She ground her teeth together and opened the lid. Did she really want to do this? An inner voice seemed to be urging her on. With trembling hands she withdrew a white Bible, which had her mother's name engraved in gold letters on the front cover. A burgundy bookmark hung partway out, and Sinda opened it to the marked page. "Psalm 19:12. 'Who can discern his errors? Forgive my hidden faults,' " she read aloud. She could hardly believe it was the same verse Glen had quoted to her the other day. "Mother must have felt guilty about something," she muttered. *Was Glen trying to tell me that I shouldn't feel guilty about anything, or was he referring to Dad? God knows, he had plenty to feel guilty about, but he always made me feel remorseful because I reminded him of Mother.*

Sinda closed the Bible and placed it on the chair next to the jewelry box and clothes. She reached inside the trunk and withdrew a small, black diary. It was fastened with a miniature padlock, but Sinda knew she could easily pry it open.

She went downstairs to the kitchen and took a pair of needle-nosed pliers from a drawer, then dropped to a seat at the table. In short order she had the lock open. *Would this be considered an invasion of privacy?* she wondered. *How could it be? Mother's gone, and after what she did to Dad and me, I have every right to read it.*

She opened the dairy to the first entry, dated October 30, just a few days after Sinda's third birthday. With one hand cupped under her chin, she began to read.

Dear Diary:
  Today I received some wonderful news. A visit to the doctor confirmed my suspicions—I'm pregnant again. The baby is due the middle of April. It will be nice for Sinda to have a sibling. Another child might be good for our marriage too. William was thrilled with the news. He wants a boy this time.

Sinda felt a headache coming on, and she began to rub her forehead in slow, circular motions. "Mother was pregnant when I was three years old? I'm an only child. What happened to the baby?"

She read on, finding the next entry dated several months later.

Dear Diary:
  Christmas is behind us for another year. This was probably one of the happiest holidays we've ever had. We had friends over for dinner, and all William could talk about was the child we're expecting in the spring. Sometimes my husband can be a bit harsh, but I'm hoping our baby will soften his heart.

The pain in Sinda's head escalated, and she wondered if she should quit reading and go to bed. A part of her wanted to escape from the past, but another part needed to know what happened to the child her mother had carried—the one her father hoped was a boy; so she read on.

Dear Diary:

My heart feels as though it is breaking in two. A terrible thing happened, and I wonder if I'll ever recover from the pain. I gave birth to William Shull Jr. one week ago, but he lived only three days, never leaving the confines of his tiny incubator. The child was born two months prematurely, and William is inconsolable. He blames me for the baby's death and says I did too much during my pregnancy. He's convinced that if I'd rested more the child would not have come early.

Sinda covered her mouth with her hand as she choked on a sob. She'd had a baby brother! A child she'd never met and had no memory of. That in itself was painful, but the stark reality of her father wanting a son and blaming her mother for denying him the right was a terrible blow. She wrapped her arms around her stomach and bent into the pain. "Could this have been the reason Mother left?" she moaned. As the thought began to take hold, she reminded herself that she'd been ten years old when her mother abandoned them. That was seven years after William Jr. died. There had to be some other reason Mother had gone. Sinda was sure her only hope of discovering the truth lay in her mother's diary. She would get to the bottom of it, even if it took all night!

❧

Sinda read the diary until the early morning hours, but the impact of her mother's final entry had been too much to bear. She'd fallen asleep on the couch, with the diary draped across her chest.

A resonant pounding roused her from a deep sleep. The

diary fell to the floor as she clambered off the couch and staggered to the front door in a stupor. She wasn't aware that she'd spent the night in her blue jeans and sweatshirt, or that her eyes were bloodshot and her hair a disheveled mess until she glanced at her reflection in the hall mirror.

She opened the door and was surprised to see Glen standing on the front porch with a desperate look on his face. "Glen, what is it?"

His forehead wrinkled. "I need a favor, but I can see by looking at you that you're probably not the best one to ask."

"I didn't sleep well last night," she stated flatly.

"I'm sorry. Why didn't you call?"

She shrugged. "I'm fine now. What do you need?"

"A baby-sitter."

"What?" She stared at him blankly, trying to force the cobwebs out of her muddled brain.

"I need someone to watch Tara," Glen explained. "Mrs. Mayer phoned early this morning. She's sick with the flu."

"Won't Tara be in school all day?"

Glen shook his head. "She's off for the summer."

"Oh, I forgot." Sinda ran her fingers through her tangled hair, wishing she hadn't answered the door. "There's no point in you losing a whole day's pay. Send Tara over."

"I would have asked Penny's mother, Gwen, but they're on vacation at the beach this week. So if you're sure it wouldn't be too much of an inconvenience, I'd really appreciate your help today."

Of course it was inconvenient, but she would do it. Glen had done her plenty of favors, so turnabout was fair play. "It's fine. I had a bad night, but it won't keep me from watching Tara."

Glen's worried expression seemed to relax. "Thanks so much, Sinda." He touched her shoulder lightly. "How about coming over for supper tonight? I'll make my famous pasta, and I could fix a Caesar salad to go with it."

She reached up to rub the side of her unwashed face. "You're not obligated to cook for me, Glen. After walking your mail route all day you shouldn't have to come home and cook for me, anyway. Why don't you come over here tonight? I'll do the cooking."

"Are you sure you don't mind?"

She pushed an irritating lock of hair away from her face. "Positive."

He grinned. "You're wonderful. I'll send Tara over right away."

Glen leaned toward Sinda, and she thought he might be about to kiss her. She pulled quickly away when she remembered she hadn't yet brushed her teeth. "No problem. See you later."

He hesitated a moment, then with a wave of his hand, Glen turned and left. Sinda closed the door with a sigh, wishing she had time to shower and change before Tara arrived. A quick trip to the bathroom to wash her face and run a brush through her unruly curls was all she was able to manage before she heard another loud knock.

When Sinda opened the door Tara thrust a piece of paper into her hand. "Dad told me to come over here for the day and said I was supposed to give you this." The child was wearing a white blouse under a pair of green overalls, and she held a silver skateboard under the other arm.

Sinda motioned her inside and glanced at the document. It was a form giving Sinda permission to authorize emergency medical care for Tara. Great. "Uh, I'd rather you not do any skateboarding today."

Tara frowned. "Why not? I skateboard all the time."

"I know. I've watched you out front, and you've taken a few spills. You're in my care today, so I won't be responsible for you getting hurt."

Tara ambled into the living room and flopped onto the couch, wrapping her arms tightly around the skateboard, as though it were some kind of lifeline. "You're not my mother, you know. I don't have to do what you say."

Sinda felt her irritation begin to mount. She'd discovered

some terrible things yesterday, spent a restless night on the couch, had been awakened by a desperate man, and now this? She was near the end of her rope, and one more good tug would probably cause it to snap right in two. She clenched her teeth and leveled Tara with what she hoped was a look of authority. "Your dad asked me to watch you today. This is my house, and I'll make the decisions. Is that clear?"

Tara nodded and dropped the skateboard to the floor. "What am I supposed to do all day?"

"Maybe we can work on some dolls." Sinda feigned a smile. "You did such a good job helping before."

Tara shrugged. "I never did anything that great. Besides, dolls are for kids."

"No, they're not," Sinda countered. "Lots of grown women, and even some men, collect dolls. Some are worth a lot of money. As you well know, many of the ones I repair are for collectors and antique dealers."

"I saw your picture in the paper a few weeks ago," Tara said, changing the subject. "That must have been really great for business."

Sinda nodded. "It was good advertisement. Several people have brought in dolls they want restored for Christmas."

"Christmas is a long ways off."

"Some dolls need lots of work. It takes time to repair them."

Tara wrinkled her nose. "People give away old dolls as presents?"

"Often a parent or grandparent will have a doll from their childhood that they want to pass on to a younger family member." Sinda took a seat in the overstuffed chair directly across from Tara. *I wonder if the girl knows anything about the doll her father asked me to fix.* "Did your mother have any dolls?" she casually questioned.

The child shrugged her shoulders. "I wouldn't know. I was only a year old when she died. I thought you knew that."

Sinda felt her face flush. Of course she knew it, but she wasn't about to tell Tara why she was fishing for information.

Learning whether she knew about the doll wasn't all she planned to fish for, either. Since she had Tara alone for the day, maybe she could ask her some questions that would give an accurate picture of the way Glen was at home, when no one could see if his mask of Christianity had slipped or not.

"All I have are some pictures to prove that my mother even existed," Tara went on to say. "To tell you the truth, I don't feel like I ever had a mother."

"I know what you mean," Sinda said softly. "As I told you before, I lost my mother when I was young."

Tara didn't seem to be listening anymore. She was looking at something lying on the floor next to her skateboard. She reached down to pick it up. "What's this—some kind of diary?"

Sinda jumped up. "Give me that!" She snatched the book away so quickly that Tara's hand flew up, and she nearly slapped herself in the face.

"Hey, what'd you do that for? I wasn't gonna hurt the dumb thing!"

Sinda snapped the cover shut and held it close to her throbbing chest.

"What's in there?" Tara squinted dramatically. "Some deep, dark secrets from your past?"

"It's none of your business! Diaries are someone's private thoughts, and this one is not for snoopy little girls!" Sinda bolted for the door. "I'm going upstairs to take a shower. You can watch TV if you like." She stormed up the steps, painfully aware that it was going to be a very long day.

seventeen

It was almost six o'clock when Glen arrived at Sinda's for supper. Her hair was piled up on her head in loose curls, and she was wearing a long, rust-colored skirt with a soft beige blouse.

Glen gave a low whistle when she opened the door. "You look great!"

She smiled and felt the heat of a blush creep up the back of her neck. "A far cry from the mess that greeted you at the door this morning, huh?" Sinda was feeling a bit friendlier toward Glen this evening. After questioning Tara today about her dad, she'd learned that he had never been physically abusive. If anything, Glen was sometimes too permissive which explained why Tara got away with being so sassy.

Glen reached for her hand. "I know you don't always sleep in your clothes. Can you tell me about it now?"

"Not this minute." Sinda motioned toward the living room where Tara sat, two feet from the TV set.

Glen nodded. "You're right. Little pitchers have big ears, and mine probably holds a world record." He followed Sinda into the kitchen. "What's on the menu?"

"Lasagna." She opened the oven door to take a peek at its progress.

He sniffed the air appreciatively. "It smells terrific."

"I hope it's fit to eat," she said. "I found the recipe in a magazine, and it said not to precook the noodles, so I can only hope it'll be all right."

"Even if the noodles turn out chewy as rubber bands, I won't care." Glen's voice dropped to a whisper, and he moved closer. "Have you been praying about us?"

Sinda edged away from him, until her hip smacked the edge of the cupboard. "Ouch!"

He pulled her quickly into his arms. "Are you okay?"

She tried to push away, but her backside was pressed against the cupboard, and she had no place else to go. Her heartbeat picked up speed, and her mind became a clouded haze as he bent to kiss her. *Glen is a great dad; Tara said so today. Glen is a good neighbor; his actions have proven it to be so. Glen is a wonderful kisser. . .*

"No! No kissing!"

Glen and Sinda both whirled to face Tara.

"Young lady, that's enough!" Glen's face was red as a cherry, and a vein on the side of his neck bulged slightly.

Tara lifted her chin defiantly. "Can we go home now?"

"No, we certainly cannot go home! I just got here, and Sinda's worked hard to fix us a nice supper. We're going to sit down and enjoy the meal, just like any normal family."

What does a normal family look like? Sinda wondered. Appearances had always been so important to her father. She and Dad used to look like the picture of happiness, and she was sure everyone at their church had thought they were content. *If they'd only known what went on in our home.*

Tara's reply broke into Sinda's troubling thoughts. "We're not a family. I mean, we are, but Sinda's not part of it."

"I'm hoping she will be someday," Glen announced.

Sinda's mouth dropped open, and Tara began to cry. "Don't you love me anymore, Dad?"

Glen left Sinda's side and bent down to wrap his arms around Tara. "Of course I love you, but I also love Sinda."

"Why?" Tara wailed. "Why do you love her?"

Glen glanced over at Sinda, and she gripped the edge of the cupboard for support. "Sinda is a beautiful, sweet lady," he said, nodding toward her.

Sinda's ears were burning. Glen was telling Tara things she had no right to hear. Especially when they weren't true. She wasn't sweet. She had bitterness in her heart and wasn't able to trust. Besides, even if Glen was all he appeared to be, and even if she were able to set her fear of hurting him aside, Tara was still an issue. The child didn't like sharing her father, and Sinda was sure Tara would never accept the fact that Glen was in love with her. There was no future for her and Glen. Not now, not ever.

❧

Sinda pulled back the covers and crawled into bed as a low groan escaped her lips. The last twenty-four hours had felt like the longest in history—her history, at least. It had begun with the reading of her mother's Bible and diary. Next, her day had been interrupted and rearranged when Glen showed up on her doorstep needing a baby-sitter for his inquisitive child. Then Tara had taken up most of her day with nosey questions and a bad attitude. The final straw came in the kitchen, where Glen professed his love for her in front of Tara. The child's predictable reaction nearly ruined dinner, even if the lasagna had turned out well. Glen and Tara went home shortly after the meal, and Sinda had been grateful. At least she wasn't forced to tell Glen what was troubling her so much that she'd slept on the couch in her clothes last night.

Sinda tucked the sheet under her chin and shifted her body to the right, then the left, trying to find a comfortable position. "I can't have a serious relationship with Glen, no matter how much my heart cries for it."

Sinda had never known the heady feeling of being in love before, and even though she found it exhilarating, she couldn't succumb to it. She was scared of marriage. She'd spent her whole life afraid of her father, blocking out his verbal and physical abuses by telling herself that even if he was doing wrong, she deserved it because she was like her mother. She'd convinced herself that Dad was the way he was because of the pain Mother had inflicted on him. Sinda had vacillated between blaming her mother, her father, and even herself. She knew the truth now, though—her mother's diary had finally brought everything into focus.

Sinda turned her head to the right, and her gaze came to

rest on the diary, lying on the bedside table. She was thankful Tara hadn't read any of it. She reached out and grabbed it, thumbing through several pages, forcing herself to read her mother's final words one more time.

Dear Diary:
William and I had another argument. He continues to blame me for the death of our son, even though it's been two years. He wishes we'd never married and says even the sight of me makes him sick.

"Were you sickened by the sight of me, Dad?" Sinda whispered into the night. She sniffed deeply and forced herself to read on.

What did I do to cause William to feel such animosity? He even said he and Sinda would be better off without me. I love my daughter, and I can't bear to think of leaving her. Besides, where would I go? How would I support myself? I have no relatives to turn to, and no money of my own. William handles all the finances. I'm only allowed enough cash for household expenses. If I need personal things or clothes for Sinda, I have to make an itemized list, then he decides how much I'll be allowed to spend. William makes good money at his accounting firm, yet he acts as though we are paupers.

Sinda felt a knot form in her stomach as she tried to visualize her mother begging for money. The poor woman must have had no self-esteem. *Of course, I had no self-esteem when Dad was alive, either. If I had, I'd have left home and made a life of my own. Instead, I felt obligated to take care of Dad and try to make up for what Mother did to him.* Tears slipped from her eyes and landed on the next entry.

Dear Diary:

    William's abuse has escalated. Last night, during another heated argument, he hit me. I didn't see it coming in time, so the blow landed on my jaw. It left an ugly bruise, and this morning I can barely open my mouth.

    Thankfully, Sinda was asleep when it happened. I hope she never discovers the awful truth about her father. She seems devoted to him, and he to her.

A sob ripped from Sinda's throat, and tears coursed down her cheeks. "It's true, Mother. My loyalty was always with Dad. I did everything he told me to do. I remember hearing the two of you arguing, but I refused to accept what was really happening." She drew in a deep breath and turned to the last entry in her mother's diary.

Dear Diary:

    I know what I must do, and it's breaking my heart. It's been seven years since William Jr.'s death, yet I've been reminded of it nearly every day. My husband won't let me forget, nor will he quit laying the blame at my feet. He's become more and more physically abusive, and I fear for my life. William gave me an ultimatum last night. He said I must move out of our house and leave Sinda with him.

    I've become William's enemy, and it seems as if he wants it that way. I've tried to reestablish what we once had, but he's built a wall of indifference and hatred around himself. I've seen a counselor and even suggested that we try to have another baby, but he won't hear of it. He says I had my chance and failed. He insists that I take on a new identity and begin another life. One that won't include my precious little girl. He says that I have no other choice, and if I refuse, he'll tell Sinda I killed her baby brother. She's too young to understand. I'm afraid she would side with her father.

    He said that if I don't leave, he will force me to watch

while he doles out my punishments to Sinda. After suffering years of his abuse, I know well what William is capable of doing. I would do anything to protect our daughter.

Sinda's throat felt constricted, and it became difficult to swallow. "Oh, Mother, why didn't you tell me the truth? Or why didn't you at least take me with you? You left me with a bitter, angry man." She shook her head slowly. She'd practically idolized her father when she was a child, and even if her mother had told the truth, she wouldn't have believed it. Dad had said everything was Mother's fault, and Sinda had accepted it as fact.

"I didn't see the truth because I didn't want to," she moaned. "Dad was more of a hypocrite than I'd ever begun to imagine!" She blinked away her tears, as she continued to read.

I've decided I must go in the morning, before Sinda wakes up. I'll leave a note on the kitchen table, stating only that I'm leaving and will never return. God forgive me for not having the courage to stand up to William. I have no family living nearby, and I don't even know if I can support myself. Taking Sinda with me would be a selfish thing to do. As much as I'll miss her, I know she will be better off with her father.

Sinda drew in a shuddering breath and tried to free her mind of the agonizing pain that held her in its grasp. "Dad used to tell me I would end up like you, Mother. I only dated a few times, and never more than once with the same man. Dad convinced me that, should I ever marry, I'd end up hurting my husband the way you hurt him." She covered her face with her hands and sobbed. Like mother, like daughter. Her father's accusing words rang in her head as she rocked back and forth, clutching a pillow to her chest. She'd lost so much. If only she'd been able to see through her father's charade. If she could just go back and change the past. Was it possible that Dad really had repented that night at the revival service? Why had he told Alex Masters to see that Sinda was given her mother's trunk? Could Dad have been trying to make restitution?

Sinda knew that only God could have seen what was in her father's heart. What mattered now was what she planned to do with her future. She hadn't known Glen very long, but in the short time they'd been together, she knew one thing for certain. She loved him as much as she was capable of loving anyone.

eighteen

Sinda awoke the following morning feeling groggy and disoriented. A barrage of troublesome dreams had left her mind in a jumble. She forced herself to shower and change into a pair of blue jeans and a white T-shirt. There were several dolls that needed to be finished, and she knew staying busy would be the best remedy for her negative thoughts and self-pity.

She and Tara had done some work in the basement yesterday. Since nothing unusual had happened, she'd talked herself into going back down there again today. She had to conquer her fears, and facing them head-on was the only way.

After breakfast Sinda cleaned up the kitchen, made a few phone calls to customers, balanced her checkbook, took out the garbage, fed the dog and cat, and watered all her houseplants. By the time she finished her chores, it was noon and she was ready for lunch. This gave her an excuse to put off going to the basement awhile longer.

Panther rubbed against Sinda's leg as she stood at the kitchen sink, peeling a carrot to add to her shrimp salad. The cat purred softly when she lifted her foot to rub the top of his sleek head with the toe of her sneaker. "Would you like to go downstairs with me?" she murmured.

The feline meowed and turned so she could rub the other side of his body. Sinda was glad Panther had come to live with her. He'd already proven to be quite the mouser. No more strange noises in the basement, and no more jumping doll parts! Sinda had been hoping her two pets would become friends, but so far it didn't appear as if that would happen. She tried to keep them separated as much as possible, alternating Sparky and Panther from the house to the yard. She probably should find another home for one of them, but right now she had more pressing matters to worry about. The first one—to get some dolls ready to go home.

A short time later, Sinda flicked the basement light on and proceeded into the doll hospital. She had little enthusiasm, but at least she was going to get something accomplished.

Sinda knew she'd become good at her craft, but on days like today she had little energy, limited confidence in her abilities, and no feeling of self-worth. In fact, she wondered if her life had any meaning at all. Where would she be living and what would she be doing twenty years from now? Would she still be here in this old house, stringing dolls, gluing on synthetic wigs, and pining for a love she could never have? Except for Carol, she had no real friends, although Glen wanted to be her friend. In fact, he wanted more than friendship.

Before she abandoned me and Dad, I thought Mother and I were friends, Sinda thought wistfully. She massaged her forehead with the tips of her fingers, hoping to halt the troubling thoughts. *I wonder if Mother's still alive. It's been almost twenty-three years since she left. Would it be a mistake to try to look for her after all this time?*

"Maybe I'm not her only daughter. If Mother took on another identity, she might have gotten married again and could even have a whole new family by now. She's probably forgotten she ever had a daughter named Sinda." She moaned and shook her head. "And what would I say if I found her?"

As intriguing as the idea was, because of Dad, Sinda felt sure her mother would want nothing to do with her. Mother no doubt thought Sinda was on his side. After all, during the time her mother had been living with them, Sinda and her father had been close. *Does Mother even know that Dad is dead?*

Sinda pushed all thoughts of her mother aside and forced her mind to focus on the Raggedy Ann doll, whose face was missing its black, button eyes. In short order she completed the job of sewing on new eyes, then she went to work on an old composition baby doll. One leg was missing, so Sinda rummaged for the part in a box marked Composition Doll

Legs. She searched thoroughly, knowing there had been a match the last time she looked.

"I can't figure it out," she fumed. "I showed Mrs. Allen the leg I'd be using as a replacement the day she brought the doll in. Where could it be?"

Thinking she might have taken it out earlier and placed it somewhere, Sinda looked on all the shelves and through every box of composition parts. When she still couldn't locate the leg, she set the doll aside to work on something else.

Another doll needed a new wig. Her old one was made of mohair and had been badly moth-eaten. Sinda opened the top drawer of an old dresser used exclusively for doll wigs. She knew the right size and color would be there because she'd recently received an order from one of her suppliers. She searched through every package of wigs, but couldn't find the one she needed. "I don't understand this!" She slammed the drawer shut with such force it caused the drawer below to fly open.

Sinda gasped. Wedged between two boxes of open-and-close eyes was a vinyl doll arm. It was the one she'd been looking for the other day, when Glen helped her search for missing doll parts. "What in the world is going on?"

Icy fingers of fear crept up her spine as she closed the drawer then opened the one below. She kept stringing-cord in several sizes here, along with wooden neck buttons used on the older bisque dolls. Lying in the middle of a coil of elastic cord was a composition doll arm. It was also one she had been looking for.

"I've got to get out of here!" Sinda banged the drawer shut and bolted for the stairs. A few minutes later, she stood in the kitchen, willing her heartbeat to return to a normal, steady rhythm. She wiped her clammy hands on the front of her jeans and sank wearily into a chair. Leaning both elbows on the table, Sinda let her head fall forward into her hands.

Several minutes later, she lifted her head and glanced at the clock above the refrigerator. It was only three o'clock. Glen wouldn't be home for at least two hours. Sinda shook her head. *Why am I thinking of him?*

"Maybe a nap will help," Sinda mumbled. She left the kitchen and curled up on the couch in the living room, with Panther lying at her feet.

For the first half hour, sleep eluded her. Fears and troubled thoughts hissed at her like corn popping over hot coals. "Help me, Lord. Please help me." The words exploded in her head, as she realized that she was praying. Maybe she hadn't strayed as far from the Lord as she'd thought. Maybe He did still care about her.

When Sinda finally fell asleep, her thoughts mingled with her dreams and she could no longer distinguish between what was real and what wasn't.

Glen. . .

Tara. . .

Missing dolls. . .

Mother. . .

Sinda was awakened to the resonating chime of the grandfather clock, letting her know it was half past five. She sat up, yawned, and stretched like a cat. "Some little nap we took, huh, Panther?" The cat didn't budge, so she left him alone on the couch.

Her stomach rumbled as she plodded toward the kitchen. "I think I'd better have something to eat."

Her nerves were a bit steadier now, though she still felt physically fatigued and mentally drained. Some nourishment would hopefully recharge her batteries and get her thinking clearly.

Sinda opened the refrigerator to get some milk for the makings of clam chowder. She picked up the carton and halted. Her world was spinning out of control. With a piercing wail, she dropped the milk to the floor, turned, and rushed out the back door.

❧

Glen was standing at the stove frying lamb chops for supper

when he heard a sharp rapping on the door. Knowing Tara was engrossed in her favorite TV show in the living room, he turned the burner down and went to see who it was.

When he opened the door, startling green eyes flashed with obvious fear, and Sinda practically fell into his arms. He held her for several seconds, letting her wet the front of his T-shirt with her tears. When he could stand it no longer, Glen pulled back slightly. "What is it? Why are you crying?"

"I think I'm going crazy!" Sinda shifted her weight from one foot to the other, and he noticed how badly she was trembling.

"Come, have a seat at the table." Glen led Sinda to the kitchen, offered her a chair, then handed her a napkin. "Dry your eyes, take a deep breath, and tell me what has you so upset."

"Remember the missing doll parts we hunted for the other day?" she asked, her voice quivering.

He nodded and sat down beside her.

"I found some of them today."

"That's great! See, I told you not to worry."

She grasped his arm. "It's not great! I found the parts accidentally—in some really weird places!"

She went on to give him the details, and he listened quietly until he thought she was finished. "I still don't see why you think you're going crazy. We all misplace things. The other day I lost my car keys again, and Tara found them lying on the living room floor."

"It's not the same thing. I haven't even told you the worst part."

"There's more?"

She lowered her gaze to the table. "I was about to fix some chowder for supper, and when I opened the refrigerator to take out the milk, I found a doll body—one that's also been missing." She sucked in her lower lip. "It wasn't there earlier when I fixed lunch. Do you see now why I think I'm losing my mind?"

"I'm sure there has to be some logical explanation," he said with an assurance he didn't really feel.

She looked at him hopefully. "What do you think it is?"

He reached for her hand and gave it a gentle squeeze. "I don't know."

She hung her head dejectedly, and it pulled at his heartstrings. What was there about this woman that made him want to protect her? Was it the tilt of her head, that cute little nose, those gorgeous green eyes, her soft auburn hair? Or was it Sinda's vulnerability that touched the core of Glen's being? Had God sent her to him, or was it the other way around? Perhaps they needed each other more than either of them realized.

Glen shook his thoughts aside and focused on Sinda's immediate need. "Why don't you stay here for supper? Afterward, we'll go back to your house, and I'll help you look for more doll parts, or at least some clues that might tell us something about what's been going on."

Sinda raised her head. "Thanks, but I have to tell you, I don't have much hope of finding anything."

He studied her face a few seconds. Her smile was the saddest one he'd ever seen. It nearly broke his heart to see her suffering like this.

Prayer. That's what they both needed now. Lots and lots of prayer.

nineteen

"Why can't I come, too?" Tara whined after Glen informed her that he was going over to Sinda's house.

"Because you have dishes to do."

"There aren't that many," she argued. "I could do them when we get back."

Since when is Tara so anxious to go to Sinda's? Glen wondered. *She's got to be up to something. He pointed to the sink.* "I want you to do the dishes now, Tara."

Tara's lower lip protruded. "Please, Dad."

"Pouting will not help."

"Maybe we could use some help on this case," Sinda suggested. "After all, Tara has been practicing to be a detective."

The child jumped up and down excitedly. "A case? What kind of case are we on?"

"We are not on any case," Glen answered firmly. "I am going to help Sinda look for a few things she's misplaced." He turned, so only Sinda could see his face, and he held one finger to his lips. When she nodded, he faced Tara again. "If we run into problems we can't handle, I'll call you."

"Promise?"

"I said so, didn't I?"

Before the child could reply, Glen grabbed Sinda by the hand and led her out the back door.

"Are you sure you have time for this?" Sinda asked when they reached her back porch.

"I'll always make time for you." Glen's answer was followed by a quick kiss.

"I wish you wouldn't do that."

He wrapped his arms around her. "You mean this?" When he bestowed her with another kiss, he noticed she was blushing.

138

"I think we'd better go inside. Our neighbors might get the wrong idea." Sinda opened the back door and motioned toward her kitchen floor. "Excuse the mess. When I saw the doll body in the refrigerator, I dropped a carton of milk. I was so scared, I just ran out the door." She grabbed some paper towels, then dropped to her knees.

Glen skirted around her, heading for the refrigerator. Sure enough, there was a pink doll body lying on the top shelf. He reached inside and pulled it out, hardly batting an eyelash over this latest phenomenon.

"Be careful with that," Sinda cautioned. "It's quite valuable."

He carried it gingerly across the room and placed it on the table.

She stood up and moved to his side. "So what do you think?"

Glen drew in a deep breath. "I'd say someone is playing a pretty mean trick on you, and I've got a good idea who that someone might be."

"You do?" She clutched his arm as though her life depended on it. "Who is it, Glen? Who could be hiding my doll parts?"

"My daughter."

Sinda's eyes widened. "You think Tara did it?"

"She's the only one with opportunity or motive."

"You make it sound as though she's some kind of a criminal."

He shrugged. "I wouldn't put it quite like that, but Tara does resent you. I think finding out I'm in love with you might have pushed her over the edge." He cleared his throat a few times. "Now you know why I didn't want her coming over here yet. I needed to discuss this with you in private." He wiped his forehead with the back of his hand. "Of course, she is the only one who can help us find the rest of the missing doll parts."

Sinda stood there, slowly shaking her head. "But how? When could she have done all this?"

"When she was helping you repair dolls," he answered. "She was here for several hours at a time, then again when you kept her while Mrs. Mayer was sick."

Sinda pulled out a chair at the table and almost fell into it. "I did catch her nosing around the place a few times, while she was helping out with the dolls." She clicked her tongue. "I can't believe Tara would do something so cruel."

"Was she ever alone? Were you out of her sight long enough for her to hide the parts?"

"Several times, but—"

Glen snapped his fingers. "Case solved!" He pulled out the chair next to Sinda and took a seat.

"It's not as simple as you might think," Sinda said, toying with a strand of her hair.

"It seems like an open-and-shut case to me. The only thing left to do is have a little heart-to-heart talk with that daughter of mine."

She touched his arm. "Tara was not in my house today, Glen."

"So?"

"She couldn't have put the bisque doll in my refrigerator."

Glen squeezed his eyes shut, praying for guidance as he tried to put the pieces of the puzzle together. "Maybe she did it yesterday."

Sinda shook her head. "The doll wasn't there before my nap. Tara hasn't been here today, and neither has anyone else."

Glen's forehead wrinkled. "I'll tell you what I think."

"What's that?"

"I think the doll body was in the refrigerator earlier, and you just didn't see it."

"I don't think so," she argued. "If it had been there, I'm sure I would have noticed."

He pursed his lips. "I'm convinced that Tara has something to do with this. She could have come over here while you were taking your nap. Was the back door unlocked?"

Sinda shrugged her shoulders. "I don't know. I usually lock it, but it's possible that I forgot after I took out the garbage."

"If the door was unlocked, Tara could have come inside, crept down to the basement, picked up the doll body, and put it in your refrigerator." Glen turned his hands palms up. "It makes perfect sense to me. Tara's jealous and she's taking it out on you."

Sinda's body sagged with obvious relief, and she gave him a wide smile. "Glen Olsen, you're beginning to sound more like a detective than your nosey daughter." She emitted a small sigh. "If you're right about this, and Tara is responsible, what do we do now?"

He stood up. "I'm going to call my detective daughter on the phone and tell her to get over here right now."

"Could you wait awhile on that?"

"What for?"

"I'd like to discuss a few other things. That is, if you have the time to listen."

Glen chuckled in response to her question. "For you, I have all the time in the world."

❧

Sinda handed Glen a glass of iced tea as they took a seat on the couch in her living room. She was about to bare her soul, because she couldn't carry the pain any longer. Her nerves were shot, her confidence gone, and she was afraid she might be close to a complete mental breakdown. "You know that old trunk of my mother's?" she asked as she pushed a stack of magazines aside and set her glass down on the coffee table.

Glen nodded.

"I looked through the rest of it the other day, and I found her Bible, as well as an old diary."

"Have you read any of it?"

Her eyes filled with unwanted tears. "All of it."

"I assume the content was upsetting?"

Sinda reached for her glass and took a sip of tea before answering. "Terribly upsetting."

"Is that what you wanted to talk about?"

She swallowed hard and nodded. "Remember when I told you that Mother left when I was ten years old?"

"I remember."

"Her diary revealed some things I didn't know before.

Some alarming things." Sinda paused and licked her lips. "Mother didn't leave because she wanted to. She was forced to go."

Glen's eyebrows shot up. "Forced? How so?"

"When I was three years old, Mother had a baby boy, but he was born prematurely and died a few days later. If not for that diary, I would never have known I'd even had a brother." Tears coursed down Sinda's cheeks, and she wiped them away with the back of her hand. "Dad blamed Mother for the death of the baby."

Glen frowned as he set his glass of tea down on the table. "I don't understand. How could your mother be held accountable for a premature baby dying?"

"As far as I can tell, she wasn't responsible. Her dairy says Dad accused her of doing too much while she was pregnant. He hounded her about it for years—even to the point of verbal and physical abuse."

"Your dad must have wanted a son badly to be so bitter and hostile. I think he needed professional help."

Sinda closed her eyes and drew in a deep breath. "He took me to church every Sunday and claimed to be a Christian."

"Just because someone goes to church doesn't make him a Christian. Christianity is a relationship with God." Glen flexed his fingers. "Far too many people go to church only for show."

She nodded in agreement. "I was shocked to learn it was Dad's blackmailing scheme that drove Mother away." Sinda choked back the sob rising in her throat.

Glen's eyes clouded with obvious confusion. "Blackmailing?"

Sinda set her glass down on the coffee table and stood up. She began to pace the length of the room. "Apparently Dad demanded that Mother move away and take on a new identity. He threatened to tell me that she'd killed my baby brother if she didn't." She hung her head. "He also threatened to hurt me."

When Glen stood up and guided her to stand in front of the fireplace, she leaned her head against his arm. "I can't believe I was so taken in by his lies. If I had only known the truth."

"You were just a child. Children usually believe what their parents tell them, whether it's right or wrong."

Sinda's eyes pooled with a fresh set of tears. "I grew up thinking I was just like my mother, and Dad reminded me of it nearly every day."

Glen quickly embraced her. "You can't let the words of a bitter, hateful man control your life. God created you, and He gave you the ability to love and be loved."

"I can't," she sobbed. "After what Dad did, I can never trust another man."

Glen kissed her forehead. "You can trust me."

"I wish it were that simple."

"It can be. Let me help you, Sinda. Let me show you how much I care."

She moved away from him. "I need more time. I need to work through all the things I've just learned. Dad pretended to be such a good Christian, all the while blaming Mother for everything. He was abusive to her, and as much as I hate to admit it, there were times when he abused me." She shuddered. "It was not normal discipline, Glen, but hair pulling, smacks across the face, a belt that could connect most anywhere on my body, and once, he even choked me."

Glen's eyes darkened. "I'm beginning to understand your reluctance to let me get close," he said, resting his forehead against hers. "I'm so sorry for all you've been through."

She sniffed deeply. "I've never discussed this with anyone. Our family secrets were well hidden. No one knew how controlling Dad could be." The strength drained from Sinda's legs, and she dropped into a nearby chair. "I covered for him because I thought everything was Mother's fault. If she hadn't gone, he might have been kinder. If I hadn't reminded him of her, maybe. . ." Her voice trailed off, and she closed her eyes against the pain.

Glen snorted. "Each of us is responsible for our own actions, and not all men are like your father." He moved to stand behind her, then began to knead the kinks from her shoulders and neck. "You've been through so much and discovered a lot in the last few days."

She shivered involuntarily. "There's still the matter of the missing doll parts. The mystery hasn't been solved yet, and until it is. . ."

"It will be solved soon," Glen said with assurance. "By the end of this evening, we'll have some answers."

twenty

When Tara arrived at Sinda's, she was wearing a satisfied smile, but Glen glared at her, and it quickly faded.

"What's wrong, Dad? I thought you called me over to help solve a case."

He ushered Tara into the living room and motioned her to take a seat, then he joined Sinda on the couch.

"What's up?" Tara asked, dropping into the antique rocker.

Seconds of uneasy silence ticked by, then Glen glanced at Sinda. "Do you want to tell her or shall I?"

She shrugged. "She's your daughter."

Glen leaned forward, raked his fingers through his hair, then stared at Tara accusingly. "Sinda has some doll parts that are missing. Would you care to tell us where they are?"

Tara rapped her fingers on the arm of the chair. "Where were they last seen?"

Glen jumped up and moved swiftly across the room. "Don't play coy with me, young lady. You know perfectly well where they were last seen. Tell us where they are now!"

Tara's mouth dropped open, and her eyes widened. "You think I took some doll parts?"

"Didn't you?"

She shook her head.

"Come on, Tara! This has gone on long enough! Sinda needs those parts, and I want you to tell her where they are!"

Feeling a sudden need to protect Tara from her father's wrath, Sinda stood up and knelt in front of the child's chair. Even if Glen wasn't going to strike his daughter, he was yelling, and that upset her. "We're not mad at you, Tara," she said softly.

"Speak for yourself!" Glen shouted.

Tara looked up at her father, and her eyes filled with tears. "I haven't done anything wrong, and I don't know a thing about any missing doll parts."

"Are you saying you haven't hidden doll parts in some rather unusual places?" Sinda asked.

"Like maybe a freezer or the refrigerator?" Glen interjected.

Tara's mouth was set in a thin line. "I don't know what you're talking about."

"Tara Mae Olsen, I'm warning you. . . ."

"Maybe she's telling the truth," Sinda interjected.

Glen shook his head. "She has to be the guilty party. She's the only one with a motive."

"What kind of motive would I have?" Tara asked shakily.

"Do you really have to ask? You're jealous of Sinda, and you're trying to scare her away with ghost stories and disappearing doll parts."

Sinda looked the child full in the face. "Please believe me, I'm not trying to come between you and your father."

Tara glared back at her. "I think you've got him hypnotized into believing he loves you."

Glen held up his hands. "See, what'd I tell you? She hid those doll parts out of spite!" He gave Tara another warning look. "Are you going to show us where they are or not?"

The child squared her shoulders. "I can't, because I don't know."

"I believe her, Glen," Sinda said as she pulled herself to her feet.

"Well, I don't, and if she doesn't confess, she's going to be punished!"

Sinda flinched. She closed her eyes, trying to dispel the vision of her father coming at her with his belt. *You're a bad girl—just like your mother, and you deserve to be punished.* Dad's angry words echoed in Sinda's head, as though he were standing right beside her. She cupped her hands against her ears, hoping to drown out the past.

Sinda felt Glen's hand touch her shoulder. "I'm sorry. I'm a little upset with my daughter right now, but I shouldn't be snapping at you."

When Sinda made no reply, he added, "It's okay. No one's going to get hurt." He gave Tara an icy stare. "Even if they do deserve to be spanked."

Tara shrugged, apparently unconvinced of the possibility of being taken over her father's knee. "I can't make you believe me, but I am a good detective. So if you'd like my help solving this mystery, I'm at your service."

Sinda offered the child what she hoped was a reassuring smile. "We appreciate that."

"Where do we start?" Tara asked eagerly.

"I think we should wait until tomorrow," Glen said. "It's getting late, and we'll all function better after a good night's rest."

Sinda gulped. "You might be able to get a good night's rest, but I sure won't. I haven't slept well in weeks. Not since this whole frightening mess started."

"I've got an idea. Tara and I can spend the night over here," Glen suggested. "That way you won't be alone."

Before Sinda could respond, Tara grabbed her father's arm and begged, "You've got to be kidding!"

Glen brushed her hand aside. "I'm completely serious. You can sleep upstairs in one of Sinda's spare rooms, and I'll sleep down here on the couch." He smiled at Sinda. "Since tomorrow's my day off, and Tara's on summer vacation, we can sleep in if we like. I'll fix us a hearty breakfast, and afterward we'll turn this house upside down until we find all those doll parts. How's that sound?"

It sounded wonderful to Sinda, but she hated to admit it. "I–I couldn't put you out like that, Glen."

"I'm more than happy to stay." He glanced down at Tara, who stood by his side with a frown on her face. "Let's think of this as an adventure. Who knows, it could even prove to be fun."

❧

Sinda sat on the edge of her bed with her mother's diary in

her lap. She blinked against the tide of tears that had begun to spill over. *Mother, if you are still alive, where are you now? Do you ever think of me? Have you tried to get touch with me?* She didn't know why she kept running this over and over in her mind, or why it seemed so important to her now. She glanced at the diary again and knew the reason. *Mother didn't leave because she wanted to. She left because she was afraid of Dad. She thought he would turn me against her, and she was right, that's exactly what happened.* Thoughts of her father's betrayal seemed to be just under the surface of her mind, like an itch needing to be scratched, and she groaned.

Throughout her youth, Sinda's resentment toward her mother had festered. It wasn't anger she was feeling now, though. It was sadness and a deep sense of loss, but she knew there was no going back. What was in the past was history. She would have to find the strength to forgive both of her parents and move on with her life.

She snapped off the light by her bed and collapsed against the pillow. What she needed now was a long talk with her Heavenly Father, followed by a good night's sleep.

&

Glen punched his pillow for the third time and tried to find a comfortable position on the narrow couch he was using as a bed. He hoped they would find some answers to the doll mystery soon. Sinda needed to feel safe in her own home. He didn't relish the idea of making her living room a permanent bedroom every night, either. He gave the pillow one more jab and decided he could tough it for one night.

Glen fought sleep for several hours, and just as he was dozing off, a strange noise jolted him awake. He glanced at the grandfather clock across the room, noting that it was one in the morning. He sat up and swung his legs over the edge of the couch. His body felt stiff and unyielding as he attempted to stretch his limbs. He listened intently but heard no more noises. Since he was already awake, he decided to get a drink of water.

Glen entered the kitchen and was about to turn on the faucet at the sink when he heard the basement door open and click shut. He whirled around in time to see Sinda walk into the room. He hadn't turned on the light, so he could only make out her outline, but it was obvious that she was wearing a long nightgown. She padded across the room in her bare feet. It looked like she was holding something in her hands.

Glen squinted, trying to make out what it was. "Sinda? What are you doing?"

She made no reply as she bent to open the oven door.

"You're not planning to do any middle-of-the-night baking, I hope," he teased.

When she still didn't answer, he snapped on the overhead light. "What on earth?" Sinda was putting a vinyl doll leg into the oven! He moved in for a closer look, watching in fascination as she closed the oven door and turned to leave.

Glen followed her through the hallway. She opened the door that led to the basement and descended the stairs in the dark. Afraid she might fall, he turned on the light over the stairwell and followed.

Sinda walked slowly and deliberately into the doll hospital, apparently unaware of his presence. Glen watched in amazement as she pulled one of the boxes from a shelf and retrieved a small composition arm. She set the box on her workbench, turned, and made her way back to the stairs. When she reached the top, she headed toward the next flight of steps.

Glen stayed close behind, holding his breath as Sinda entered the guest room where Tara lay sleeping.

Sinda walked over to the dresser, bent down, and opened the bottom drawer, then placed the doll arm inside. When she banged the drawer shut, Tara bolted upright in bed. "Who's there?"

"It's me, Tara," Glen whispered. "Me and Sinda."

Tara snapped on the light by her bed. "What's going on, Dad? What are you doing in my room in the middle of the night?"

"Go back to sleep. I'll explain everything in the morning."

Glen took Sinda's hand and led her toward the door.

"Wait a minute!" Tara called. "If something weird's going on, I want to know about it! After all, I was forced to spend the night in this creepy house, and I'm supposed to be helping you solve a big mystery."

Glen nodded. "You do deserve an explanation, but now's not the time. I need to get Sinda back to her own room."

"What's she doing in here again?"

Glen's forehead wrinkled. "Again? What do you mean?"

"She was in here earlier. I asked what she wanted, but she didn't answer. She walked over to the window, stood there a few minutes, then left. It was really creepy, Dad."

Sinda stood there, staring off into space and holding Glen's hand as though she didn't have a care in the world. Glen glanced over at her before he spoke to Tara again. "I think Sinda's been sleepwalking," he whispered. "I found her in the kitchen, then followed her to the basement."

"What was she doing down there?"

"Getting a doll part. She put one in the oven, and just now she placed a doll arm in that drawer." He pointed to the dresser and frowned.

"How weird!" Tara exclaimed. She nodded her head toward Sinda. "Just look at her. She's staring off into space like she doesn't know where she is."

"She doesn't," Glen said. "She has no idea what she's done, or even that she's out of her bed."

"Then wake her up."

"I don't think that's a good idea. I heard somewhere that waking a sleepwalker might cause them some kind of emotional trauma." He glanced at Sinda again, feeling a deep sense of concern. "I don't know if it's true or not, but to be on the safe side, I think I'll wait and tell her in the morning."

Suddenly Sinda began swaying back and forth, hollering, "Oh, my head! It hurts so bad!"

Glen held her steady, afraid she might topple to the floor.

She blinked several times, then looked right at him. "Glen?

What are you doing in my room?"

"This isn't your room," he answered. "It's the guest room."

Sinda's face was a mask of confusion. "I'm in the guest room?"

He nodded. "I followed you here. You were sleepwalking."

๛

Sinda sat at the kitchen table, holding a cup of hot chocolate in one hand. "I still can't believe I'm the one responsible for all those missing doll parts." She looked over at Glen, who sat in the chair beside her. "Do you think I'm losing my mind?"

He reached out and took hold of her free hand. "No, but I believe you're deeply troubled about that diary you found in your mother's trunk."

Sinda feigned a smile. "I don't think I've ever walked in my sleep before. In fact, the doll parts didn't turn up missing until that stupid trunk arrived. Maybe that's when all the sleepwalking began."

She saw Glen glance at the clock across the room. It was nearly two in the morning. Tara was back in bed, but Sinda needed to talk, so Glen had suggested they come to the kitchen for hot chocolate.

"Sinda," Glen said hesitantly, "I know you're upset about your recent discoveries, and I think maybe your subconscious has chosen to deal with it in a rather unusual way."

Sinda blew on her cocoa before taking a tentative sip. "I'll bet there are doll parts hidden all over this house. How am I ever going to make it stop happening?" A sickening wave of dread flowed through her. She looked at Glen, hoping he could give her some answers. "I can't go on living like this. Doll repairing and selling antiques is my livelihood. I can't keep losing doll parts or wandering around the house at all hours of the night like a raving lunatic."

"You're not a lunatic," Glen said softly. "I think the best thing for you to do is try to put the past behind you and start looking to the future."

"The future?" she shot back. "Do I even have a future?"

A tear trickled down her cheek, and Glen dried it with his thumb. "Of course you have a future. One with me, I hope."

Sinda rested her head on his shoulder and a low moan escaped her lips. "I only wish it were that simple."

"It can be," he whispered.

She lifted her head. "You have a spirited daughter to raise, Glen. Do you really want to take on the responsibility of baby-sitting your neurotic neighbor?"

Glen graced her with a tender smile. "It would give me nothing but pleasure."

"What about Tara?"

"What about her?"

"She doesn't like me. And this discovery won't help."

Glen leaned over and gently kissed her. "She'll grow to love you as much as I do." He wiggled his eyebrows. "Well, maybe not quite that much."

Sinda smiled in spite of her nagging doubts. She glanced at the clock again. "I've kept you up half the night. I'm sorry for causing so much trouble."

"I'd do it all over if you'd promise to think about a future with me," he said.

She studied him intently, realizing he had a much softer heart than she'd ever imagined. "You're serious, aren't you?"

"Couldn't be more serious." He drew her into his arms. "I don't want to rush you into a relationship you're not ready for."

"Thanks," she murmured. "I've still got a lot of things to work out."

"I'm here if you need me, and when the time's right, I hope to make you my wife."

Her eyes filled with tears. "You'd be willing to marry a crazy sleepwalker who can't deal with her past?"

He snickered. "I'm not worried about that. I think as you begin to trust God fully and let Him help you work through the pain, there'll be no need for your nightly treks."

"I hope you're right, Glen," she murmured. "I really hope you're right."

twenty-one

For the next several weeks, things went better. Sinda was able to locate most of the missing doll parts, her sleepwalking had lessened, and Tara, though reluctantly, did seem a bit more resigned to the fact that Glen and Sinda planned to keep seeing one another. Sinda and Glen had gone to a couple of yard sales, and they'd even taken Tara on a picnic at the lake. They had also started praying regularly and studying the Bible together several evenings a week.

Sinda's biggest hurdle came when she agreed to attend church with the Olsens on the first Sunday of August. Today would be the first time she'd been in church since her father died, and just the thought of it set her nerves on edge. Would she fit in? Would the memory of Dad and his hypocrisy keep her from worshiping God?

She stood in front of the living room window, waiting for Glen to pick her up, and when she closed her eyes briefly, she could see her father sitting in his church pew with a pious look on his face. "How could I have been so blind? I knew how harsh Dad was with me. Every sharp word. . .every physical blow. . . Why didn't I realize he'd been the same way with Mother? Why did I blame her for his actions?"

A knock on the front door drew Sinda away from the window. Glen was waiting. It was time to go to church.

❧

Sinda glanced over at Glen, then past him to Tara, who sat on his other side. He was smiling and nodding at the pastor's words. An occasional "Amen" would escape his lips. Was Glen really all he seemed to be? How could she be sure he wasn't merely pretending to be a good Christian, the way her father had? Could she ever learn to fully trust again?

153

"God's Word says, 'Don't worry about anything; instead, pray about everything. Tell God what you need, and thank him for all he has done..' " Pastor Benton's quote from Philippians 4:6 (NLT) rocked Sinda to her soul. She'd spent so many years worrying about everything, praying about little, and never thanking God for the answers she'd received to those prayers she had uttered. Hadn't it been God, working through Glen, who showed her the facts regarding the missing doll parts? Hadn't she learned the truth about her mother because God allowed her the opportunity to read that diary?

The pastor's next words resounded in her head like the gong of her grandfather clock. "In Hebrews 11:1 we are told that faith is being sure of what we hope for and certain of what we do not see. The sixth verse of the same chapter reminds us that without faith it's impossible to please God." Pastor Benton looked out at the congregation. "How is your faith today? Are you sure of God's love? Have you put your hope in Him? Are you certain of the things which you cannot see?"

Sinda knew her faith had been weak for a long time. She'd allowed her father's deceit and abusive ways to poison her mind and cloud her judgment. She couldn't trust men because she hadn't been trusting the Lord.

As though he sensed her confusion, Glen reached over and gave her hand a gentle squeeze. She smiled and clasped his fingers in response. It was time to leave the past behind. Sinda was ready to look to the future and begin to trust again. She felt an overwhelming sense of gratitude to God.

❧

The pungent, spicy smell of Glen's homemade barbecue sauce simmering in the Crock-Pot permeated the air as Sinda and Glen entered his kitchen after church. Tara was out in the living room watching TV, and Sinda was glad they could be alone for a few minutes. "Need help with anything?" she asked.

He nodded toward the nearest cupboard. "I guess you can set out some paper plates and cups while I start forming the hamburger patties and get the chicken out of the refrigerator."

Glen headed for the refrigerator, and Sinda moved toward the cupboard he'd indicated. They collided somewhere in the middle of the room, and Glen quickly wrapped his arms around her. "Hey, I could get used to this kind of thing," he murmured.

She smiled up at him. "You think so?"

"Does this answer your question?" He bent his head, and his lips eagerly sought hers. The kiss only lasted a few seconds because they were interrupted by a deep voice.

"Ah-ha! So this is how you spend your Sunday afternoons!"

Sinda pulled away and turned to see Glen's brother standing inside the kitchen doorway, arms folded across his broad chest and a smirk on his bearded face.

"Phil! How'd you get in here?" Glen asked, brushing his fingers across his lips.

"I came to the front door, and Tara let me in. The kid said you were fixing hamburgers and chicken to put on the grill, but it looks to me like you were having dessert." Phil chuckled and winked at Sinda. Her face flamed, and she turned away.

"If you'd been in church this morning I might have asked you to join our barbecue," Glen said in a none-too-friendly tone.

The day Phil delivered her screen door Sinda had noticed the tension between the brothers, and she'd wondered what caused it. After hearing Glen's comment about church, she surmised that the problem could be about Phil's lack of interest in spiritual things.

"I was forced to go to Sunday school every day until I moved out of Mom and Dad's house, so I'm not about to spend all my Sundays sitting on hard pews, listening to doom and gloom from a pastor who should have retired ten years ago," Phil said with a sweeping gesture.

Glen made no comment, but when Sinda chanced a peek at him, she saw that his face was flushed.

Phil sniffed the air. "Something sure smells good. How about inviting me to join your little barbecue, even if I was a bad boy and skipped church this morning?"

Glen marched over to the cupboard and withdrew a glass pitcher and a jar of pre-mixed tea. He handed it to Phil. "Here, if you're going to join us, you may as well make yourself useful."

⁂

As Glen flipped burgers on the grill, then checked the chicken on the rack above, he felt a trickle of sweat roll down his forehead and land on his nose. It was a warm day, and the barbecue was certainly hot enough to make a man perspire, but he knew the reason he felt so hot was because he was irritated about his brother joining them for lunch. Ever since Phil had shown up unannounced, he'd been hanging around Sinda, bombarding her with stupid jokes, and dropping hints about taking her out sometime. If Glen hadn't been trying to be a good Christian witness, he'd have booted his brother right out the garden gate.

Tara seemed to be enjoying her uncle's company, but Glen wondered if she was really glad to see Uncle Phil—or was she delighting in the fact that he was keeping Sinda away from her dad?

The meat was done, and Glen was about to tell his guests they could sit at the picnic table when he saw Sinda move toward the gate that separated their backyards. Was she leaving? Had she had all she could take of Phil the Pill?

He set the platter of chicken and burgers on the table and followed her. "Sinda, where are you going?"

She turned to face him. "I think I heard a car pull into my driveway. I'd better see who it is."

"I'll come with you," Glen offered.

She eyed him curiously. "Don't you want to stay and entertain your brother?"

"Phil's a big boy. He can take care of himself until we get back."

She shrugged, opened the gate, and Glen followed her around front. A sporty red car was parked in Sinda's driveway, and an attractive woman with short blond hair was heading toward the house.

"Carol!" Sinda waved. "What are you doing here?"

"I stopped by to see if you wanted to go to the mall, and maybe stop by my favorite pizza place for something to eat afterward."

"Actually, I was next door, about to sink my teeth into a juicy piece of barbecued chicken." Sinda gave Glen a quick glance, then swung her gaze back to her friend. "I guess you two haven't met."

"Not in person, but if this is the handsome mailman I've heard so much about, then I feel like I already know you," Carol announced.

Glen bit back the laughter bubbling in his throat. So Sinda had been talking about him. He smiled at Carol and extended his hand. "I'm Glen Olsen."

"Carol Riggins. It's nice to finally meet you."

"Carol and I have been friends since we were children," Sinda said. "Carol went to college while I stayed home repairing dolls and catering to my dad. Shortly after her graduation she moved from Seattle to Elmwood, and she's been after me to move here ever since."

"I'm glad you were finally persuaded," Glen said, placing his hand against the small of Sinda's back.

Carol started moving toward her car. "I should probably get going. The mall will only be open until six, and I don't want to keep you from your barbecue."

"Why don't you join us?" Sinda turned to face Glen. "You wouldn't mind one more at the table, would you?"

"I've got plenty of everything so you're more than welcome, Carol," he eagerly agreed.

Carol smiled. "I appreciate the offer, and I gladly accept."

A few minutes later, Carol and Phil had been introduced, and everyone was seated at the picnic table. Glen said the blessing, then passed the plate of barbecued chicken to his guests.

&

Sinda bit into a juicy drumstick and smacked her lips. "Umm. . . this is delicious."

"Dad can cook just about anything and make it taste great," Tara put in.

"He certainly did a good job with this," Carol agreed. "Everything from the potato salad to the baked beans tastes wonderful." She giggled and poked Sinda in the ribs with her elbow. "Don't look any deeper, 'cause this one's a keeper."

Sinda smiled and nodded. She couldn't agree more.

"Dad, where's the mustard?"

"Oops, I must have forgotten to set it out. Guess you'll have to run inside and get the bottle out of the refrigerator."

Tara's frown deepened. "How come I always have to do everything?"

"You don't have to do everything, Tara." Glen pointed toward the house.

Sinda jumped up. "I'll get the mustard."

"That's not necessary, Sinda," Glen said quickly.

Sinda held up hand. "It's okay. I'm happy to go."

Once inside the house, Sinda went immediately to the kitchen and retrieved a squeeze bottle of mustard from the refrigerator. *At least there aren't any doll parts in here,* she thought ruefully. She closed the door and moved over to the window that overlooked the backyard. She didn't see Glen sitting beside Tara anymore and figured he'd probably gone back to the barbecue for more meat. Much to her surprise, Carol had moved from her spot and was now seated beside Phil.

Sinda smiled. "Maybe Phil's found another interest. That should take some of the pressure off me. Guess Carol showing up was a good thing."

"You're right, it was. Now I don't have to share you with my woman-crazy brother for the rest of the day."

Sinda whirled around at the sound of Glen's voice. She clasped her hand against her mouth. "Glen, I didn't hear you come in!"

He grinned, and her heart skipped a beat. "I thought you might need help finding the ketchup."

"It's mustard," she said, holding up the bottle.

"Oh, right." Glen moved slowly toward her, and Sinda could hear the echo of her heartbeat hammering in her ears.

Glen bent his head to kiss her, and she melted into his embrace. "I want to marry you, Sinda Shull," he murmured.

She licked her lips and offered him a faint smile. "I–I–don't know what to say, Glen."

He gave her a crooked smile. "How about, 'Yes, I'd be happy to marry you?' "

She studied his handsome face, but before she could open her mouth to respond, there was a high-pitched scream, followed by, "Dad, you can't marry Sinda!"

Sinda and Glen both turned to face Tara. Her face was bright red, and her eyes were mere slits. "Can you give me one good reason why I shouldn't marry her?" Glen asked.

Tara marched across the room and stopped in front of her father. "Yes, I can."

Sinda knelt next to Tara. "Listen, Tara, I—"

"Dad's gotten along fine without a wife for nine whole years, and he doesn't need one now," Tara shouted. "Especially not some sleepwalking, doll-collecting weirdo!"

A muscle in Glen's jaw quivered. "Tara Mae Olsen, you apologize to Sinda this minute!"

"It's okay, Glen," Sinda said, standing up again. "She needs more time."

Tara stomped her foot. "I don't need more time. I do not want a mother, and Dad doesn't need a wife!" She pivoted on her heel and bolted for the hall door, slamming it with such force that the Welcome plaque fell off the wall and toppled to the floor.

Glen cleared his throat. "That sure went well."

Sinda's eyes filled with unwanted tears. "We'd better face the facts, Glen. It's not going to work for us. Tara isn't going to accept me."

He shrugged. "I think she's simply jealous. I'm sure she'll calm down and listen to reason."

Sinda dropped her gaze to the floor. "What if that never happens?"

He gave her shoulder a gentle squeeze, but she could see a look of defeat written on his face. "Guess I'll have to deal with it."

"Sorry about the barbecue being ruined, but I think I'd better go home so you can get things straightened out with Tara."

"I'll talk to her and try to help her understand."

Sinda blinked back her tears of frustration. She doubted that anything Glen had to say would penetrate Tara's wall of defense. She hated to admit it, but there was no future for her and Glen Olsen. Just when she'd made peace with God and had begun to trust, the rug was being yanked out from under her. Would she ever know real joy? Was it even possible to experience the kind of love God planned for a man and a woman?

twenty-two

Glen found Tara in her room, lying across the bed, crying as if her heart were breaking. He approached her slowly. "Tara, I need you to listen to me."

"Go away."

"I'm in love with Sinda. Won't you try to understand?" He took a seat on the edge of her bed and reached out to gently touch her back.

She jerked away. "Do you love her more than me?"

"Of course not. I love her in a different way, that's all." Glen sighed deeply. "It's been nine years since your mother died, and—"

Tara sat up suddenly. "Did you love her?"

"Connie?"

Her only reply was a curt nod.

"Of course I loved her. When she died, I thought I'd never recover, but God was good, and He filled my life with you."

She sniffed deeply. "Then how come I'm not enough for you now?"

Several seconds passed, as Glen tried to come up with an answer that might make sense to his distraught daughter. "God's plan was for a man to have a wife," he said softly. "I've waited a long time to find someone I could love enough to want for my wife."

Tara jumped up and stalked over to the window. She stood there, looking out at Sinda's house. "If you marry her, it'll never be the same."

"Tara, I know—"

She reeled around to face him. "I could never love Sinda."

How could he choose between Sinda and his daughter? He was in love with Sinda, but Tara was his only child. Until Tara calmed down and they worked through her jealousy, he'd have to keep Sinda Shull at arm's length. He hoped she would understand, but could he ask her to wait?

&

Sinda moped around the house for the next several weeks, unable to get much work done or even fix a decent meal. She'd heard from Carol, with news that she and Phil had gone bowling. This should have brought her joy, since it obviously meant Phil's interest had shifted from her to Carol. However, Glen had called too, informing her that he'd tried to reason with Tara, but it was to no avail. The child wouldn't accept the prospect of their marriage. Sinda understood, but the question foremost on her mind was what to do with the rest of her life. Even though Glen had tried to convince her that Tara would come around someday, she knew in her heart that their romance was over.

As she stood there staring out the living room window, Sinda caught a glimpse of the man she loved leaving for his mail route. She'd never meant to fall in love, and every encounter with Glen was something she both dreaded and anticipated. How could she stand seeing him like this, knowing they had no future together? Each time they met and uttered a casual greeting, a part of her heart crumbled a bit more. Sinda wanted to jerk the front door open and call out to Glen, but she knew it would be a mistake. She couldn't live here any longer, hoping, praying things would change. She wasn't growing younger, and she had no desire to wait around until Tara matured.

"The best thing I can do is move out of this house and get as far away from Elmwood, Oregon, as possible," she muttered. As soon as she had some breakfast, Sinda planned to phone the Realtor. *No point putting off until tomorrow what you can do today.* Her father's favorite expression rang in her ears. This time, however, she would do it because it was the only way, not because it was something Dad would have expected.

It was nearly noon when Sinda called the Realtor's office,

but she was informed that the Realtor who'd sold her the house was on vacation and wouldn't be back for two weeks. Sinda could either call someone else or wait.

"Guess a few more weeks won't matter," she muttered as she hung up the phone. "It will give me a chance to spruce the place up a bit so it looks more appealing to any prospective buyers."

Sinda left the kitchen and went out front to do some weeding. The flower beds were in terrible shape, and she knew a thorough going over should help. Dropping to her knees, with a shovel in her hand, Sinda filled her mind with determination. She glanced up when she heard laughter. Tara and her friend Penny were skateboarding on the sidewalk in front of her place. They had made some kind of crazy ramp out of plywood and a bucket. Penny waved, but Tara didn't even look her way.

A pang of regret stabbed Sinda's heart as she was reminded of how much she had lost. Not only had she been forced to give Glen up, but she'd been cheated out of having a stepdaughter. If only she and Tara could have become friends.

Sinda thrust the shovel into the damp soil, forcing her thoughts back to the job at hand. It would do no good to think about the what-ifs.

A verse of Scripture she'd read that morning popped into her mind, and she recited it. " 'And we know that in all things God works for the good of those who love him, who have been called according to his purpose,' Romans 8:28." Surely God had something good planned for her. It simply wasn't going to be here, in this neighborhood, in the town where Glen Olsen lived. She'd have to move on with her life, even if it meant going back to Seattle, where she was born and raised.

Another thought came to mind. If she did go home, maybe she could discover the whereabouts of her mother. Perhaps she was still living in Seattle. Sinda knew she was grasping at straws, but in her present condition, she needed something to hang on to.

She grabbed a handful of weeds and gave them a yank. It felt good to take her frustrations out on the neglected flower bed. Half an hour later, she'd finished up one bed and was about to move to another when she heard a scream.

Her head snapped up. Sparky, who'd been lying peacefully at her side, ran toward the fence, barking frantically.

Sinda scrambled to her feet and followed the dog. She was surprised to see Tara sprawled on the sidewalk. Her skateboard was tipped on its side, a few feet away.

With no hesitation, Sinda jerked the gate open and hurried down the steps. Tara's friend Penny was standing over Tara, sobbing hysterically. "I only gave her a little push down the ramp, and I didn't mean for her to get hurt."

Sinda moved Penny gently aside and knelt next to Tara. Her eyes were shut, and she was moaning. "What is it, Tara? Where are you hurt?" She couldn't see any blood, yet it was obvious from the agonized expression on the young girl's face that she was in a great deal of pain.

When Tara spoke, her words came out in a whisper. "My head. . .my arm. . .they hurt." She opened her eyes, then squeezed them shut again.

Sinda's mouth went dry. One look at the girl's swollen, distorted-looking wrist told her it was most likely broken. She knew how to put broken dolls back together, but she didn't know the first thing about giving first aid to an injured child. Sinda looked up at Penny, who was still whimpering. "Penny, go tell Tara's baby-sitter to call 9-1-1. Tell her I think Tara has a broken arm and could have a concussion."

"Tara's staying at my house this week while her dad's at work."

"Then ask your mother to call for help."

Penny muttered something about it being all her fault, then she bolted across the street. Sinda leaned closer to Tara. "It's going to be okay. The paramedics will be here soon."

"Don't leave me," Tara wailed. "Please don't go."

An onslaught of tears rolled down the child's pale cheek,

and Sinda wiped them away. "I won't leave you, Honey, I promise."

❧

As Sinda began to pace the length of the hospital waiting room, the numbness she'd felt earlier began to wear off. Penny's mother offered to call the post office to see if they could track Glen down, and Sinda had been allowed to ride with Tara in the ambulance. Once Glen arrived, Sinda had taken a seat in the waiting room.

She had just picked up a magazine when a nurse stepped to her side. "Are you Tara Olsen's baby-sitter?"

"I'm their next-door neighbor. Why do you ask?"

"Tara asked me to come get you," the nurse said. "She wants both you and her dad to be there when the doctor sets the bone."

The room began to spin, and Sinda closed her eyes for a moment, hoping to right her world again.

"The X-rays confirmed she broke her wrist," the nurse explained.

"Does she have a concussion?"

The nurse shook her head. "She's one lucky girl. I've seen some skateboard accidents that left the victim in much worse shape. Kids sure don't know the meaning of the word careful." She patted Sinda's arm in a motherly fashion. "It's a good thing you were there when it happened."

"I was only doing the neighborly thing," Sinda said absently. Her brain felt like it was on overload. Tara's wrist was broken, the doctor was about to set it, and the child wanted her to be there.

Sinda squared her shoulders and followed the nurse down the hall.

twenty-three

It was the last Saturday of October, and today was Sinda's thirty-third birthday. She found it hard to believe how much her life had changed in the last few months. Everything wasn't perfect as far as her emotional state, but thanks to God's love and Glen's friendship, she was beginning to heal. She was confident that the days ahead held great promise.

As Sinda checked her appearance in the full-length mirror on the back of her bedroom door, her thoughts began to drift. *I wish you were here to share in my joy, Mother. If only things had been different between you and Dad. I wish. . .*

There was a soft knock on the door, and she was grateful for the interruption. There was no point in dwelling on the past again. Not today. "Come in," she called.

Tara, dressed in a full-length, pale yellow gown and matching slippers, entered the room. Her hair was left long, but pulled away from her face with a cluster of yellow and white ribbons holding it at the back of her head.

"You look beautiful," Sinda murmured. "Just like a flower in your mother's garden."

"Thanks. You look pretty too," the child replied.

Sinda glanced back at the mirror. She was wearing an ivory-colored, full-length satin gown, detailed with tiny pearls sewn into the bodice. Her hair, piled on top of her head, was covered with a filmy veil held in place by a ring of miniature peach-colored carnations. "I'm glad you agreed to be my maid of honor. It means a lot to me," she said, moving away from the mirror.

Tara's cheeks flamed. "I suppose since you're gonna be my stepmom, we should try to help each other out." The child sniffed deeply, and Sinda wondered if she might be about to

166

cry. "Like you did the day I broke my wrist. After all, I am supposed to love my neighbor."

Sinda reached for Tara's hand, glad that the cast was off now and the wrist had healed so nicely. "Your dad loves you very much. That's not going to change because he's marrying me." She swallowed hard, hoping to hold back the wall of tears threatening to spill over. " I love you, Tara, and I'll never do anything to come between you and your father. I hope you'll give me the chance to prove that." Sinda blotted the tears rolling down her cheeks with her lace handkerchief. "I've always been more comfortable with dolls than I have with people, but I'm going to try hard to be a good wife to your dad, and I really want to be your friend."

Tara's lower lip quivered slightly. "Am I supposed to call you 'Mom' now?"

Sinda shook her head. "Sinda will be fine."

"I know it was dumb, but for awhile I thought you had Dad under some kind of spell." Tara gave Sinda an unexpected grin. "I'm sure glad you didn't talk Dad into living in this old house."

"My house will work out well for my business, but your house is a much nicer place to live." Sinda smiled. "And Sparky is getting along quite well at Carol's." She bent down and pulled a cardboard box from under the bed.

"What's in there?" Tara asked, taking a step closer.

"Something for you." Sinda placed the box on top of the bed and nodded toward Tara. "Go ahead, open it."

Tara lifted the lid, her dark eyes filled with wonder as she pulled out the restored antique doll. "It's beautiful. Was it yours?"

Sinda shook her head. "It was your grandmother's doll, and your mother wanted you to have it. It needed some repairs, so your dad brought it to me several months ago. We've been saving it for just the right time."

Tara's eyes pooled with tears as she stroked the doll's delicate, porcelain face. "I'll take good care of it."

Sinda slipped her arm around Tara's shoulders, and when the child didn't pull away, she whispered a prayer of thanks. There was another knock, and she called, "Come in."

The door opened, and Carol poked her head inside. "You two about ready? I think the groom is going to have a nervous breakdown if we don't get this show on the road." She chuckled. "No show—the groom might go."

Tara giggled as she moved away from Sinda. "Should we be mean and make Dad wait?"

Sinda shook her head. "I want to start this marriage off on the right foot. No lies, no secrets, and no tricks." She extended her hand toward Tara. "Ready?"

"Ready as I'll ever be," the child answered as she slipped her hand into Sinda's.

The ladies descended the stairs, and Sinda scanned her living room, decorated with bouquets of autumn flowers and candles in shades of yellow and orange. *Some might think this an odd place for a wedding,* Sinda thought with a smile, *but I wanted my marriage to begin in the house where I learned what trust and true love really means.*

As her gaze left the decorations, Sinda spotted her groom, dressed in a stunning black tux, standing in front of the fireplace. He looked so handsome. The minister stood on one side of Glen, and Phil stood on the other side. Tara and Carol had joined the bridal party and stood to the right of the men. Beside Sinda's friend was a petite older woman with short auburn hair, streaked with gray. Her green eyes shimmered in the candlelight, and her smile looked so familiar. Sinda swallowed against the knot that had lodged in her throat. No, it couldn't be. "Mother?" she mouthed.

The woman nodded, tears pooling in her eyes, and her chin trembling as she smiled.

But, how? When? Sinda, so full of questions, took her place beside Glen. She looked at her mother, then back at Glen, hoping for some answers.

"I'll tell you about it after the ceremony," he whispered.

Sinda could hardly contain herself. Here she was standing in the living room of her rambling old house, about to marry the most wonderful man in the world, and her mother was here to witness the joyful event. It was too much to comprehend.

Feeling as if she were in a daze, Sinda tried to focus on the pastor's words about marriage and the responsibilities of a husband and wife. She'd spent her whole life wondering if all men were alike, and now, as she repeated her vows, Sinda's heart swelled with a joy she'd never known. Glen sealed their love with a kiss, and she found comfort in the warmth of his arms.

As soon as the minister announced, "I now present to you, Mr. and Mrs. Glen Olsen," Glen grasped Sinda's hand, and they moved to the back of the room to greet their guests.

Sinda's mother was the last one through the receiving line, and she and Sinda clung to each other and wept. "How did you find me?" Sinda asked through her tears.

Her mother looked over at Glen. "I didn't. Your groom found me."

Sinda cast a questioning look at her husband. "How? When? Where?"

He lifted her chin, so she was gazing into his eyes. "I hired a detective, and he found your mother living in Spokane, where she'd moved several years ago. She didn't know your father was dead or that you'd moved away."

Sinda turned to look at her mother again, and her vision clouded with tears. "How come you never came to see me?"

Clutching Sinda's arm, she replied, "Your father threatened to hurt you if I did. He was an angry, confused man, and I was afraid to stand up to him for fear of what he might do." She sniffed deeply. "Even though William filed for divorce, I never remarried. In order to support myself, I took a job as a maid at a local hotel. I never missed any of your school or church programs."

Sinda's eyebrows furrowed. "How did you manage to see my programs and not show yourself?"

Her mother dropped her gaze to the floor. "I wore a wig

and dark glasses. Nobody recognized me, not even your father." She shook her head slowly. "I never stopped loving you or praying for you, Sinda. Please believe me, I had your best interest at heart."

Sinda was tempted to tell her mother that living with an abusive father could not have been the best thing for her, but she realized with regret that her mother had no idea Dad had mistreated her—no one else ever had. *It doesn't matter now,* Sinda mused. *I have Mother back again, and I'm thankful to God for that.* Through a sheen of tears, she smiled at Glen. "You're remarkable, and I love you so much."

He bent his head and kissed her so tenderly she thought she would drown in his love. "I wanted to give you a combined birthday and wedding present—something you would never forget." Then, taking Sinda's hand in his left hand, and her mother's hand in his right hand, he announced, "I thought it was the neighborly thing to do."

A Letter To Our Readers

Dear Reader:

In order that we might better contribute to your reading enjoyment, we would appreciate your taking a few minutes to respond to the following questions. We welcome your comments and read each form and letter we receive. When completed, please return to the following:

Fiction Editor
Heartsong Presents
PO Box 719
Uhrichsville, Ohio 44683

1. Did you enjoy reading *The Neighborly Thing* by Wanda E. Brunstetter?

   ❏ Very much! I would like to see more books by this author!

   ❏ Moderately. I would have enjoyed it more if

_____

_____

_____

2. Are you a member of **Heartsong Presents**? ❏ Yes ❏ No

   If no, where did you purchase this book? _____

_____

3. How would you rate, on a scale from 1 (poor) to 5 (superior), the cover design? _____

4. On a scale from 1 (poor) to 10 (superior), please rate the following elements.

____ Heroine		____ Plot	
____ Hero		____ Inspirational theme	
____ Setting		____ Secondary characters	

6. How has this book inspired your life?_____

_____

_____

7. What settings would you like to see covered in future **Heartsong Presents** books? _____

_____

_____

8. What are some inspirational themes you would like to see treated in future books? _____

_____

_____

9. Would you be interested in reading other **Heartsong Presents** titles? ❏ Yes ❏ No

10. Please check your age range:
   - ❏ Under 18
   - ❏ 25-34
   - ❏ 46-55
   - ❏ 18-24
   - ❏ 35-45
   - ❏ Over 55

Name_____

Occupation _____

Address_____

City_____ State_____ Zip_____

E-mail_____

Ohio

The first decade of the nineteenth century is full of promise and adventure for the infant state of Ohio. But for the three Carson sisters, it is filled with trepidation as they struggle with the loss of their parents in the battle for statehood.

What will be Kate, Annabelle, and Claire's legacy of faith and love for following generations?

Historical, paperback, 512 pages, 5 $^3/_{16}$" x 8"

❤ ❤ ❤ ❤ ❤ ❤ ❤ ❤ ❤ ❤ ❤ ❤ ❤ ❤ ❤ ❤ ❤ ❤

❤ ❤ ❤ ❤ ❤ ❤ ❤ ❤ ❤ ❤ ❤ ❤ ❤ ❤ ❤ ❤ ❤ ❤

Heartsong

Presents

Great Inspirational Romance at a Great Price!

Heartsong Presents books are inspirational romances in contemporary and historical settings, designed to give you an enjoyable, spirit-lifting reading experience. You can choose wonderfully written titles from some of today's best authors like Hannah Alexander, Andrea Boeshaar, Yvonne Lehman, Tracie Peterson, and many others.

*When ordering quantities less than twelve, above titles are $3.25 each.
Not all titles may be available at time of order.*

*H*EARTSONG ♥ PRESENTS

Love Stories Are Rated G!

That's for godly, gratifying, and of course, great! If you love a thrilling love story but don't appreciate the sordidness of some popular paperback romances, **Heartsong Presents** is for you. In fact, **Heartsong Presents** is the only inspirational romance book club featuring love stories where Christian faith is the primary ingredient in a marriage relationship.

Sign up today to receive your first set of four, never-before-published Christian romances. Send no money now; you will receive a bill with the first shipment. You may cancel at any time without obligation, and if you aren't completely satisfied with any selection, you may return the books for an immediate refund!

Imagine. . .four new romances every four weeks—two historical, two contemporary—with men and women like you who long to meet the one God has chosen as the love of their lives. . .all for the low price of $10.99 postpaid.

To join, simply complete the coupon below and mail to the address provided. **Heartsong Presents** romances are rated G for another reason: They'll arrive Godspeed!

YES! Sign me up for Heart♥ng!